TRANSCENDENT

FOR LOVE OF FAE TRILOGY- BOOK TWO

OLIVIA HARDIN

ISBN-10: 0989783855
ISBN-13: 978-0-9897838-5-9

DEDICATION

To Danny and Bonnie Sue,
for being my family, my babies and my companions
in good times and bad times.

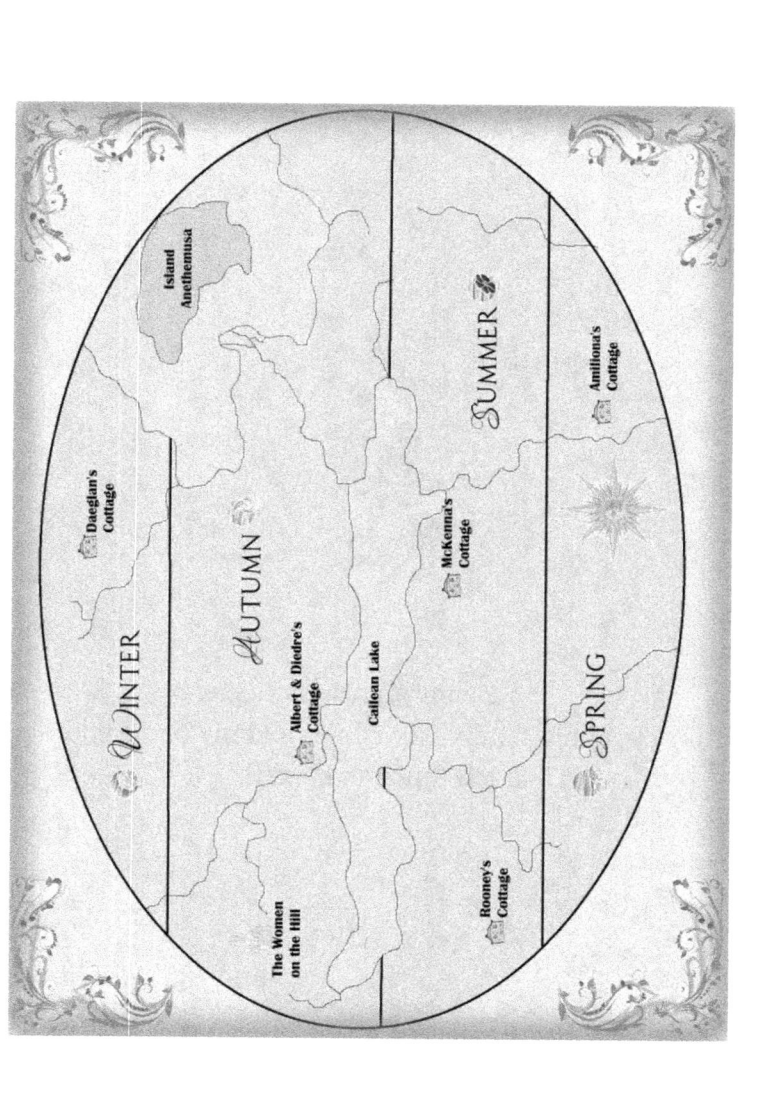

Perhaps it's age that allows me to remain patient. I wouldn't be so bold as to say I am wiser with age, but undoubtedly I am patient. Compared to the many years of my life, it hasn't really been all that long since they betrayed me. But still, it hasn't been easy to wait for my revenge.

No, no, not revenge. It can't be revenge.

That would make it wrong, and it isn't wrong. My plans are a way to reestablish the balance, to repeal the governance that puts everyone in danger.

Danger.

Danger.

Danger.

The words repeat in my head like a chant. If I say it enough, it will continue to be true.

Is it dangerous? How can I be sure? Sometimes doubt makes me want to run and hide. Sometimes I look around and see the ones inhabiting our world, and they seem so complacent. Perhaps we should just leave things as they are. No one is suffering, at least not so much. We have food, albeit we must work the land for it. We have a home that we've been able to make our own, even if they separate us from others.

No.

No.

No.

They wronged us. We protected them, provided for them, and then they betrayed us. And what about the people? They don't even know the yoke under which they labor. The menace secrets itself in nooks and crannies of their lives that they don't even know exist. One wrong move, one misspoken word, and their world could change in an instant. And no one would even know that it happened. Do ignorance, blindness make it acceptable?

The loneliness comes close to destroying me most nights. It's only the dedication to our plan that keeps me going. It is the only thing I have to live for now.

"Revenge is an act of passion; vengeance of justice. Injuries are revenged; crimes are avenged." Samuel Johnson's words were true. They have to be true.

Justice.

Justice.

Justice.

PROLOGUE

ROBBIE SCAMPERED and ran along the rubble-strewn faery realm as fast as he could. His weasel feet allowed him to leap over piles of debris and detour around rivers of water that still remained after the flooding had subsided. He counted himself lucky that he'd been able to make his way across to the Island Anethemusa and back considering how swollen the sea was.

He reached the cabin just before sunset and found McKenna pacing the room. Her expression flashed relief when she heard the clicks of his claws on the wooden floor of the porch. She slammed the door shut behind him and waited.

Her marvelous green eyes gazed down at him, wide and sparking with life. She hadn't always looked at him that way. In fact, in the early days, she rarely looked at him at all. He was a means to an end, nothing more than a pet with the very useful ability to speak.

Robbie the Weasel was a far cry from the man he'd once been. Robin Weir had been a powerful warlock, allied to the Org. He'd had everything a man could want. Influence, strength, wealth, good looks. For a while, he'd even had the beautiful faery-witch, long before anyone had even realized what she was.

But now he had none of those things.

He closed his eyes and struggled to focus on the inner light McKenna had told him about months ago. She'd been sitting with him, nuzzling his furry head and talking by the fire. She mentioned the light, and at first he couldn't figure out what the hell she meant. *It's in you. It reminds me a lot of the way faery children look when they're first coming into their magic.*

After she told him about it, he tried to figure out what it was. He studied himself, reflected on what she might have possibly seen. And one morning, just before McKenna had returned from her evening jaunt on the night wind, it happened. He closed his eyes until they hurt. He saw flashes of color behind his eyelids and he clenched his eyes harder until the color turned to bright white.

His muscles started to stretch and tear and pull. It hurt. It hurt a lot, but it felt magical, and his fascination with it was something he couldn't deny. He missed magic, and if this—whatever this was—allowed him to touch it just the slightest bit, then he wanted to embrace it even with the pain.

Now, just as then, his body shifted back into human form. He became the Robin he'd been before—or at least a shadow of that man. Reddish brown hair, keen green eyes, and a smile that sent women's hearts fluttering. He opened his eyes and saw McKenna watching him. It was hard to detect what was behind this blonde faery's gaze, but he wanted nothing more than to believe the sight of him could cause a reaction in her.

"Did you get to her?" she asked, all business as usual.

He nodded, quickly slipping into the pair of pants she always left for him on the chair beside the door. "I got across. It wasn't easy. Damned place is a mess. I told her that they brought Lodar back to the Women. She said she's not ready yet, but soon."

McKenna bit her lip and cut her eyes to the side in thought. After a moment, she shrugged, and he watched her bosom rise and fall with a deep breath. "I suppose Aoi knows what she's doing. I thought she'd be ready, but if she's not..."

He watched as his faery companion slipped out of her special sweater and allowed her wings to emerge. She liked to keep them tight against her body and warm when she wasn't flying. Night was blanketing the faery world, and the wind was beginning to whistle outside the door. That was her cue to be going.

"When this is over," he said, taking a few steps closer so she could feel his breath, "it would be nice if you wouldn't have to do this every night."

She raised a golden eyebrow, and her jade eyes glimmered. "It would be nice, wouldn't it?"

He was tempted to make a move, but she slipped past him before he could talk himself into it. McKenna was nothing if not careful. With all that was happening in the faery world, she couldn't afford to put the Women on edge by shirking her duties to them. She had a sector to keep tabs on, and until Aoi gave them the go-ahead, he would just have to settle for using the fire in the hearth to keep himself warm at night.

As always, there was a pot hanging over that fire. He approached it, rubbing his hands together above the heat for a few moments, then took a towel from a pin on the wall and used it to remove the cast-iron lid. The scent of stew wafted to his nostrils, and he closed his eyes, inhaling deep.

He was a man used to the finest cuisine. In his other life, he had dined at exorbitant restaurants, drank premium liquor, and enjoyed the high life. Now he lived in a one-room cottage, ate simple beef stew with crusty, blackened bread, and used a sweet honey mead to wash it down.

And strangely, he was okay with that. Something about this place made all of the things he used to know seem unimportant. The food, meager as it was, tasted rich and sublime. The mead warmed him, sating his mind and body so that he could relax without going straight to his head and intoxicating him.

Robin put on a long-sleeved shirt and then wrapped

a blanket around his shoulders before making himself a bowl and pulling a chair close to the fire. The Summer was normally mild of temperature, though nights were chilly. Still, since Báisteach's rage, the weather was off-kilter, and it was colder than usual.

The cottage was too quiet when McKenna was gone. Being alone was the one thing he hadn't been able to get used to here. His landlord remained above, sailing with the night wind all evening while Robin slept in her bed. At dawn, she returned, taking up his place so that she too could rest.

And when she did, he would have the chance to watch her. Peace settled into her features, and her femininity exuded from every flutter of her lashes as her eyes danced in dreams. He loved watching her sleep.

"Damn," he muttered to himself, wondering why he'd used that word—love. His past was proof enough that he didn't know about love. Even if he'd managed to learn something of it now, he knew he wouldn't deserve it. The things he'd done were unforgivable.

His mind was going to go through those things even though he wanted to clench his eyes closed and will them away. This was the real reason he hated the quiet, lonely nights. His previous life was a whirl of activity, giving him time to think only of himself and his own gratification.

Here, at night, he had to remember the things he had done. He had to mentally torture himself with the images of the children he'd sold, the blood they'd lost, the friends he'd betrayed.

All in the name of Robin Weir.

Now, Robbie the Weasel.

CHAPTER 1

Five months later

MCKENNA RAISED a long-fingered hand to hide the yawn she couldn't contain. She struggled to refrain from opening her mouth wide as tears welled in her sleepy eyes. She wasn't used to being awake this time of the morning. Her nightly flight was always long and arduous, and she liked nothing better than to climb between her blankets and let the lingering warmth left behind by Robin's body sate her into slumber.

This morning she had no choice. The Women would not have anyone missing for their grand affair—certainly not one of their *sylphe* Sentinels.

Robbie was perched on her shoulder, and when he reached a paw to scratch at his ear, the movement tickled her neck, and she shuddered as goose bumps rose on her skin. "Ahem."

His weaselly eyes gazed over at her, big and green and glistening with mirth, but he just planted his paw back onto her shoulder. "Sorry."

Every person in the faery realm was gathered at the base of the gray, silent hill for today's exhibition. It was a rare thing for the Women to call the realm together like this. In fact, it hadn't happened in McKenna's lifetime.

She managed to keep her eyes from gazing at the massive double golden doors to her left. On the other side of those doors stood the inhabitants of the Island Anethemusa, though a gauzy veil of shimmer blocked the faces. It was just as well because McKenna was afraid if she caught Aoi's gaze she might unwittingly give something away. They had come too far to let an errant look damage their cause.

"I listened around, and no one else seems to know what this is about either," Robbie whispered into her ear. "It is a complete mystery."

McKenna leaned in close to him to respond. "It isn't good, whatever it is."

It wasn't a secret that Robbie was a talking weasel. McKenna had been the one to see him cross over from the human realm. A man until he'd stepped—or stumbled—across that threshold. Then his body had shrunk immediately into his current form.

Here, it is what is. That was the mantra of things in the faery realm. Whatever Robbie had done during his human life meant that here in the faery realm he would take the form of a weasel. It was the same for Doc and Jill, Rooney's vampire friends from the other world. When they visited this place, they discarded their vampire traits and needs and became the beautiful people they truly were inside.

McKenna had, of course, reported Robbie to the Women. "He's a harmless little animal. A weasel," she'd told them. Just enough information to settle their need to know, but not enough to pique their interest. That was because when McKenna had seen him and heard him speak, she had known that she could use this particular weasel.

It was difficult to find suitable messengers to relay information between the Dissenters. No one would pay any attention to a small scurrying critter, even if he could talk.

Without warning, the ground shuddered, and a collective gasp rose up from the people. A blinding light burst from the top of the gray hill. Then the mound itself began to wobble and shake. Rolling waves cascaded down from the apex, and when McKenna looked closely, she realized the moving dirt was transporting a person trapped inside the mud.

"Lodar," Robbie breathed, and McKenna flinched in realization.

The central Woman, Báisteach, had once loved Lodar. When he betrayed her with a Siren, she'd banished him to the human world, stripping him of his powers by forcing him to cross the divide between the realms. That was when she waged a coup d'état against the royal Sirens, destroying all of them so that she could centralize control of the faery realm in the Women on the Hill.

But none of that was common knowledge in the faery realm.

And then, just five months ago, a long-lost Siren returned, crossing from the human world thanks to the faery-witch's ability to bridge the realms. Belle and Rooney had had no idea what they were unleashing when they brought her into their midst. Báisteach's rage had been virtually uncontrollable. Her sisters, the four other Women, had kept her from obliterating the entire faery kingdom until Roon and Belle could meet her demand to deliver her Lodar.

McKenna's eyes scanned the crowd for Roon and Belle but saw no sign of them. They were surely here, but with so many fae gathering in one place, it was like searching for a needle in a haystack.

"I present to you a traitor, a despot, a scourge of the faery and the human realms. Lodar was once one of us, but he could not be content with the life he was afforded here." It was Báisteach speaking, her words carrying, loud and clear, as she descended from the hill surrounded by clouds and rain and tears. She was, after all, the Woman of water, the giver of life.

McKenna kept her eyes on the vampire entangled in bonds of mud and water. He appeared sick and emaciated, but that would make sense. He was a vampire, and his true nature was that of a bloodsucking leech. The

Women would not have allowed him to feed. For five long months, he'd been held in his prison, suffering with blood starvation.

"This villain chose to become a vampire, and in his greed for power and control, he killed many of our kind. Many faeries saw their lives sucked away, including my very own son, Craig."

Of course, McKenna thought. She wouldn't tell the realm the true reasons she wanted Lodar dead. She wouldn't admit to the fact that it was her own jealousy and drive for power that had seen him sent to the human realm to have the Sirens killed off. Those were just rumors and innuendo, not sanctioned by the Women as truth.

"The death of my beloved son nearly destroyed me." Her tears increased, streaming over the crowd in misting rain. "And in my grief, I am so sorry to say that I nearly destroyed all of us. For that, I must beg your forgiveness."

She bowed her head. The falsetto contrition she displayed made McKenna want to vomit. There were murmurs from within the crowd, and she realized after a moment that some of the faeries were accepting Báisteach's appeal. In fact, some of them were begging her to take care of them, to provide as she always had.

Sheep. They were just like sheep.

"Oh, my people, my beloved people. We have recovered from the terrible storms that devastated the faery realm. We have remade our home to its glory. Now we must finish this unrest by putting an end to the source of our suffering. Justice must be served."

Shouts of accord rose up from the people, and just like a virus spreading to infect everyone within reach, the sounds of agreement trickled out until every single faery was screaming in harmony.

"Justice! Justice! Kill the traitor!"

McKenna too joined in, afraid that if she didn't someone would notice. She made the mistake of looking to the double golden doors at the people of the Island Anethemusa. Those faeries were silent, their blurred mouths held in tight lines and their brows drawn together in a collective frown.

She envied them at that moment. They were prisoners of the island, but they were free to express their dissent.

Just then, Robbie hissed, jumping onto his back feet, "Son of a bitch."

She looked just in time to see the gray hill come to life again, arms of mud reaching out on all sides. A howling wind came from every direction, and carried on that wind were shards of wood and debris, the very same debris the faeries had collected and stacked—per the Women's orders—in mounds within each seasonal sector.

Now the mud arms grabbed up thousands of pieces of wood and used them as stakes, stabbing and impaling Lodar over and over in every part of his body. The vampire screeched and howled in pain. He didn't burst into a pile of ash as vampires should. Instead, he bled out a thick, black oozing mess of fluid, his body torn and rent open in all places.

Lodar died a horrendous, painful death. Then the gray hill sucked him under, and he disappeared from sight. Everyone turned their eyes upwards, gazing as Báisteach swept her arms wide and made the misting increase to full rain, washing away the vile and nasty remnants of her former lover's blood from the hill.

The people cheered and hurrahed. But McKenna found her will to conform seep out of her. She dropped her eyes, reached up a hand to pet Robbie, and sighed. Her furry companion nuzzled his head into her palm and she drew comfort from him.

"We should go now, McKenna. You're tired."

She nodded, swallowing down the sick waves of nausea welling up in her.

Báisteach was the Woman of water, the giver of life. Today she'd showed herself to also be the taker of life.

McKenna found herself chuckling in ugly amusement. "Here, it is *not* what is," she whispered, turning so that Robbie would be the only one to hear her.

CHAPTER 2

ROBIN COULD SENSE McKenna's tension, the muscles rigid under his paws as she fought her way through the crowd to start the long trek back to her cabin. McKenna resided in the Summer, and they would have to cross the Autumn to get there. Although she had wings, she could only fly when assisted by the night wind. He imagined she could probably open a door and instantly step over to her home, but she rarely, if ever, used that particular power.

Today he figured she needed the walk to blow off some of the building emotions. He knew better than to talk about what was going on while they were out in the open. Other Sentinel faeries could be listening or watching them. That was probably be unlikely due to the faery-wide call for attendance at today's event but still not a chance he was willing to take.

After decades working with the Org, Robin knew about subterfuge.

McKenna huffed breath in and out of her nose as she raced along, her petite feet thumping across the ground with surprising heaviness. He chattered his teeth to release some of his own nerves. Within just a few moments, she side-eyed him, and he snapped his mouth shut.

"You don't have to give me that look. I'm a weasel. It's what we do." He wasn't actually sure if that was what weasels did. He wasn't even sure that he was really a weasel, just the faery version of that type of animal. Regardless, his instincts kicked in at times like this, and he almost couldn't help himself.

"I'm exhausted," she muttered, walking faster.

It wasn't exactly an apology for the nasty look she'd given him, but it was about as close as he ever got to one with her. She was prone to periods of crabbiness and melancholy. He normally told her stories and did his best to deflate the sour emotions. Before he had learned to shift into human form, he would perch on the back of her fireside chair and lightly rake his claws through her blonde hair. After he'd managed to transform into a man again, he'd use his hands to give her shoulders a massage.

An hour or so later, she pushed open the cabin door, and they entered into the safety of her home. Robbie did as he always did, leaping down off her shoulder and scurrying through the house, checking every nook and cranny for Sentinels. The most common household ones were brownies and hob elves. He was an animal with instincts for hunting small game; the small fae didn't stand a chance of hiding from him. He'd never caught one in McKenna's home, but a few times when they'd visited friends, he'd chased some of them off.

When Robbie was sure the coast was clear, he hovered near the hearth, soaking up the lingering warmth from the dying fire so that he could work himself into the change. It still wasn't easy to transform. He had to bunch his body into a ball, and for some reason, heat seemed to help him, too. He closed his eyes and searched for the internal white light, mentally sucking it into him the same way one would take in a deep breath.

He once told McKenna that the change was like turning himself inside out. He locked on to the light in his mind and squeezed and squeezed. His limbs started to stretch through the white center, and his entire body climbed out of his weasel form and into his human one.

Robin's eyes opened, and he glanced down at his naked body. He never watched the change happening, for two reasons. One, he wasn't sure if he could do it without focusing on the light behind his eyes. Two, and more importantly, he didn't really want to see his arms and legs and other parts contort from animal to human.

McKenna wasn't watching either. She was standing near the window, her body bent forward at the waist and her hands against the sill. He slipped into his clothes then brushed both hands through his reddish hair.

"Do you want to eat something?" he asked, mimicking her stance and leaning forward to clutch one of the chairs at the table.

She shook her head, blonde curls brushing to and fro against her hunched shoulders.

"If you want to try to get some sleep, I can go foraging." He didn't particularly like that idea because it would mean shifting back to weasel, and it was harder and more painful when he shifted back and forth in a short time. Still, he would do it for her. He owed McKenna for taking him in, and she rarely asked for more than he could easily give.

"Did you know him?" Her voice cracked when she spoke. She was white-knuckling the windowsill. Then, after a few moments of silence, she shoved herself upright and turned to him. The green of her eyes flashed as if on fire, and she approached the table to face him.

"Lodar?"

"You did, didn't you? You knew him."

He forced the air out of his lungs so that his torso decompressed with an arch of his back. He looked down at the table, his eyes glazing over as he relived memories that always managed to find him when he wanted nothing more than to quash them forever.

"I knew him, McKenna. So what?"

"Did he deserve that? Did he need to die?"

Robin's mind rebelled against the thoughts she recalled from him. He closed his eyes, rolled his head from side to side, and gritted his teeth.

When McKenna shoved the chair into the table, he flinched and stood upright. She approached the cupboard and started rummaging, banging things around in her agitation.

With a sigh, Robin dropped into the chair in front of him and then slapped a palm onto the table. "What the hell do you want me to say? Do you want me to say he wasn't that bad, that he was just another vampire? Would that give you enough fodder to hate them?"

The air got still, and when he glanced at McKenna, she was frozen with her hand on a ceramic mug.

"Is that what you want, McKenna? Will that ease your conscience?"

She threw the mug onto the hard dirt floor, shattering it into hundreds of shards. "I want the truth, Robin."

He chewed his tongue then swallowed and nodded. "He was a monster. A fucking demented monster. He deserves a thousand times more than what those Women gave to him."

She stared at him for a long moment, her eyes piercing into him like jade-stone knives. Then her tension dropped away and her shoulders slumped. "It doesn't make them right. This wasn't justice."

"Justice? There is no justice, McKenna. There's retribution, and it's whatever the holder of the sword wants it to be. Did I deserve to be sent through the golden door and made into a mangy weasel?"

"You're not mangy, Robin. And your life here isn't so bad. You still have your life."

He snorted, looking away. That wasn't what he meant at all. He wasn't so sure he deserved to live. He spent night after night going over what happened and wondering why Devan had seen fit to spare his life. He wasn't so different from Lodar. He was a part of the Org the same as him.

Steven Dearmon's elbow jabbed him in the ribs, and Robbie hissed and jabbed him back. "Look, man. That's him. They say he'll pay anything for the right one."

Robbie's eyes followed Landon's and caught sight of a man with confidence and power throbbing in every muscle movement entering the room. The ladies at the dinner party all eyed him, following him as he made his way through. Lodar didn't seem to care about all of the salivating women surrounding him.

"Father has a group selected especially for him. Had them tested by some of the best warlocks and then sampled by Adriel."

Robbie nodded, his gaze riveted. Something about the man made him cringe on the inside. He was said to have acquired piles of money. They said that he didn't mind handing out buckets of it for the right magical child. Robbie stuffed his hands into his empty pockets and thought of what it would be like to have even half of that kind of wealth.

His mind naturally turned to Kent and wished not for the first time in the last several years that he still had his friend and sidekick with him. They had been a strong team, Robbie and Kent, and he was sure the two of them could find a child that Lodar would be willing to pay top dollar for.

"Supposedly he doesn't use the reverie to hypnotize them. Says it dulls the taste," Landon continued with a snicker and a malevolent grin.

A shudder involuntarily shimmied down Robbie's back, and to hide the movement, he rolled his shoulders back to straighten his jacket then ran a hand through his hair. The description was a little too close for comfort. Still, the Org was his business, his family, his profession. He couldn't afford to care what that vampire did with the kids he sold to them.

"What the hell does it matter, McKenna? I'm not trying to convince you to change any of your plans. I told you the day you took me in that I'd work with you and be your eyes, ears, and feet. You and the Dissenters have my commitment. You don't need my support."

CHAPTER 3

THOUGH SHE TRIED, McKenna couldn't get any sleep. For the first thirty or so minutes, she lay completely prone under the blankets, her arm draped across her eyes. The pallet was hard and cold. Empty. Her ears could hear Robin moving around in the cabin, probably eating leftover bread and cheese.

Their earlier conversation had left her agitated and unsettled. She yearned to toss and turn with her discomfort, but she didn't want to let on to her cabin-mate how upset she really was, so she remained stone-still. Her abdomen tensed when she heard the scratching of Robbie's weasel claws on the floor, and her ears following the sound until she knew he'd hopped out the window to leave the cabin.

With a loud grunt, she rolled over onto her belly and pounded the pillow a few times. Then she folded it over and plopped her head down. She wasn't sure why the day's events had gotten to her, but her mind and heart were tied up in knots.

Robbie was here for one reason and one reason only—to be her sentry and messenger. There were eyes and ears everywhere in the faery realm. The revolution was coming, and it was difficult to relay messages between the Dissenters and especially to the fae on the Island Anethemusa. She needed Robbie to be her feet on the ground and to clear the deck when she needed to have a private conversation with one of their people.

And he was right. She didn't need him to understand the fight. She didn't need him to support her actions or those of the Dissenters. He was just a pawn she was willing to use to meet her needs.

"But dammit, I want him to understand," she breathed, burrowing her mouth into the pillow and breathing through it until the lack of good oxygen made her lungs burn. "Why should it matter if he does or doesn't?"

Robin Weir had been an Org operative all of his adult life, which, for a warlock, was a very long time. He'd sold children to vampires, made a living as a lackey to that evil trade. It shouldn't matter to him what her motives were. He was her lifeline, his means of staying alive in this world, and he would do what he had to in order to keep that line going. That was the one thing he was good at.

"That's why it matters." She silenced any further

words, knowing better than to let anything verbal slip when there might be someone listening. Her thoughts continued to churn.

Robin's opinion mattered because McKenna didn't want to just be another puppeteer pulling his strings. Her fight was right. She believed in it with all that she was, and she couldn't afford to just use him and toss him aside with no care. That was what the Women did.

And because of that, she did need him to understand. Not once had he questioned her intentions or anyone's associated with the cause. He made every run she requested without argument. He didn't ask why. She'd volunteered information, told him how the Women kept an invisible hold over all of their world and how they punished those who stepped out of line. He listened, but nothing more.

Why? Why didn't he care? Why did she want him to?

There was a little scratching sound outside the window, and McKenna hurried to a sitting position, ear cocked to listen. After a moment, she recognized the sound of something hitting the side of the cabin.

"Robbie?"

"Hey, yeah." His voice drifted up through the open window and then his furry head popped up into view. "You okay?"

McKenna closed her eyes and took a big cleansing breath. She glanced at Robbie the weasel and tried to discern what was behind those big green eyes of his. "What was that noise you were making?"

If a weasel could blush, Robbie would have. He dropped a small brown nut with a thud and ducked his head low. "I was digging a hole. Near the cabin."

McKenna wanted to laugh but sighed instead. "You don't have to bury nuts for the winter. In the first place, it's always summer in this sector. And second, we'll always have enough to eat."

Robbie shrugged and plopped down off the sill and into the house. "I know that. It's just an instinct, and my instincts go into overdrive when I'm worked up about something. And there's definitely something afoot with you right now. You're never quite this bitchy."

Raking a hand through her golden hair, McKenna lowered her eyes and moved her head up and down in agreement. "I know. I apologize. This day isn't the norm for us here and it has my nerves on edge. Let me try to get a few hours of shuteye and I'll try to be less bitchy."

Robbie winked at her with a grin. "Deal."

She hesitated before lying back down. "How would you like…maybe to go on my shift with me tonight?"

His critter eyes widened. Then he picked up the nut, lifted his paws to his mouth, and started chewing. "I suppose," he began, "I could do that. If you want."

She had to force a smile, worry churning a hole in her gut. "Okay then." And she rolled her body to face the wall, closing her eyes to find sleep.

CHAPTER 4

"**D**EAL."
Robbie slapped his hand into Kent's with a firm nod and then smiled a sly half smile. They were just teenagers, but Kent was intent on making his brother happy. He believed that if he could make Adriel proud, then his brother would give him the gift, make him a vampire, too. Robbie didn't understand his friend's desire to become a bloodsucker. That was the last thing Robbie wanted.

Vampires were black, sick, and evil. Robbie worked for them, did their bidding, but he would never become one.

"You're sure you can do it? What if they see you?"

Kent issued a slight upturn of his lips, almost a smile but not quite. "They won't notice."

The Org was in the business of selling magical children to vampires. The business was changing, picking up *speed as the market increased, and Kent's brother was intent on becoming an integral part of the organization.*

He dealt in only the best, and now that Kent was no longer young enough to be desirable as a child supplicant, he could help Adriel detect the magic in other children.

And now Kent had a lead on a special child. He needed Robbie to get him close enough to the safe house. Then he insisted that he would do the rest.

"Okay." Robbie waved his hand in front of him and a golden door opened up. This was a new trick for him. He'd learned it from another warlock and had been surprised when he first achieved it. Not everyone with magic could, Kent being one of them.

Kent leaned forward, peeking inside the doorway. "Is it the right place?"

Rolling his eyes, Robbie shoved his friend affectionately. "You gave me the directions. I know what I'm doing, and it's the right place. Get in there." He rubbed his hands together. "I'm ready to get my hands on some cold, hard cash."

He watched with some trepidation as his best friend crossed the threshold to step into an alley behind the church. Supposedly the little boy with curly black hair went there each night for a free meal. If he was as powerful as Kent said he was, it should be a very significant find for Adriel. And Kent's brother paid them well for those.

Robin woke with a start. He hadn't meant to doze off, but he figured the events of the day had put enough tension into his body that he'd needed a bit of rest too. He glanced at McKenna's pallet to find it empty. She was probably out collecting ingredients for their evening meal.

He ruffled his hand through his red-brown hair and tried to clear the fog of the dream he'd been having just before waking. It must have been his earlier talk with McKenna that had his old memories riled up. He didn't like to think of them. They were as ghosts, haunting him when he was vulnerable.

After Kent had gone through that golden door, he'd disappeared. Robin didn't see him again until the night he and his girlfriend Devan killed Adriel. There were rumors that his friend had been abducted by a shaman. Later, Kent joined the Company, a paranormal watch group. And that eventually led to his mission to do away with the Org and of course to Robin's banishment to the faery realm.

The cabin door swung open and Robin looked up to see McKenna entering, her arms laden. By the looks of it, she had some fresh cheese from their neighbors Gavin and Priscilla. The couple often shared in exchange for the fresh meat Robin often hunted. The faery realm was all about the barter system.

"I didn't catch anything for tonight," he told her. It wasn't often that he couldn't come up with at least a bird or a shrew, but the animals were skittish today, probably due to the unusual traffic of fae moving throughout the realm.

"It's fine," she said dropping the block of cheese onto the table and unwrapping the cloth from it. "There is plenty of cheese here and some sausage and fruit in this bag."

"All from Gavin?" He drew back in surprise. "I haven't provided that much game lately."

McKenna laughed, something she didn't do often, and when he gazed at her, he noticed the change in her complexion. She was pleased or excited about something. "Well, Gavin is spreading the joy. He and Scilla have some news. She's expecting."

Robin grinned. "A baby? I suppose I'll need to start providing a bit more game then."

McKenna's head bobbed. "They're thrilled. They've been married some time, and I know they've wanted a child. I think it is a long-awaited blessing."

It might have been indiscernible to most, but Robin noticed something change in her eyes. They were brilliant green, as all faeries' eyes were, but the inner light flickered behind the irises, and he could detect the worry worming back into her expression.

He moved to the cupboard to retrieve some plates and utensils. As he did, he reached out his arm and allowed his fingers to touch her shoulder then skim along her back and neck as he moved behind her. He didn't miss the shiver that passed through her body, though she'd tried to stiffen it away.

They ate in silence, but that wasn't unusual. In the early days, he had been unnerved by it, the only sound between them the movement of their jaws. Now, he found comfort. An easy understanding had developed between them in these moments. He thought maybe they were just better when they weren't confronting the issues of their past and politics.

"Almost sunset," she murmured after they'd cleaned up.

"So how do we do this?"

She studied him, her eyes narrow and intense. "You really want to come with me?"

Robin's head cocked to the side. "Of course I want to. I've been waiting for almost a year to get the invitation. Think I'm going to let you back out now? No way."

And with that, he closed his eyes, focusing on shifting out of human form. When he opened them, he was five feet shorter than he had been, his furry paws held out in front of him in wonder.

"All right then," McKenna smiled, reaching down to pick him up.

CHAPTER 5

MCKENNA USED a scarf to rig up a sling for Robbie to ride in. He insisted that it was unnecessary, but she knew the stiff winds could sometimes send her into steep dives and sharp turns. She wouldn't take the chance that he might fall off her back.

Securing him against her chest, she reached her arms out and fluttered her wings, waiting for the wind to catch her just right. Her eyes closed, she inhaled with a slow lift of her chest and tried to relax. That wasn't easy considering she had a living, breathing critter against her breast.

Not to mention, this was Robbie. The man who had shared her cabin for almost fourteen months—although the first five or so had been exclusively as an animal. But recently, he'd taken to living more as a man than a weasel, and that had her thinking more and more of him *as* a man.

He was attractive beyond compare, and the familiarity of their close living arrangement wasn't lost on her. The intimacy was especially profound considering the quick glimpses of his nude body in that moment just after shifting from weasel to human.

Now Robbie wiggled, and she would have sworn she could feel the effect of that movement radiate across her entire body. She swallowed the lump in her throat before speaking. "Hold on."

McKenna could hear the wind approaching, and she leaned in, ducking her head so that the brunt of it could catch her unfurled wings. The caress of the air skimming her body was always exquisite. She closed her eyes and enjoyed the flip-flop of her stomach as her body attained lift. For a brief moment, she hung in the air, floating over one spot. Then her body took over and her wings pressed her off into the night.

When McKenna sailed the night wind on her Sentinel journeys, she instinctively scanned the ground with her eyes, looking and watching for anything that was amiss. This night was quiet, and she thought most of the fae were likely within their homes, huddling together and working at figuring out the morning's goings-on.

Robin said something, but she couldn't understand with the wind whirling past them. He cocked his weasel head up at her and she cupped a hand to her ear to indicate she couldn't hear him.

"I said it's amazing. A completely different sensation from flying in an airplane. It's almost like we're floating."

She smiled a bit, scanning the Summer as they dipped and rose on waves of air. "We mostly are floating. My wings help me stay aloft and let me shift directions, but otherwise I couldn't do this without the night wind."

"Is there always a wind?"

There was a movement in the woods about five hundred yards from a *dryad* woman by the name of Hilda. A woodland faery, Hilda had become a widow almost fifty years earlier when her dwarf husband was killed in a hunting accident. She was a sweet woman with adult sons who took care to be sure she had everything she needed to get by.

A golden glow suddenly shone from the spot in the woods, so before answering Robin's question, McKenna shifted her body to change directions so that she could see what was happening. "There is always a night wind here. Isn't there in the human world?"

"No, not always."

Voices rose up from the illuminated place in the woods. McKenna recognized Hilda's voice and those of two males.

"You're wrong. You don't remember any such thing." Hilda shook her head and wrung her hands in front of her. "It was an accident. You were only four, Direon."

"I was four, but I remember something, Mother. The

execution"—he practically choked on the word—
"brought up some glimmer of something. He was sucked
under by the mud, Mother. I know he was."

The light Direon had fixed to a torch made Hilda's
pallid face appear green and eerie. Her eyes were wide,
haunted. She was so absolutely still that for a moment
McKenna couldn't tell that she was breathing.

"No, Direon. He was trampled by a passel of hogs.
That is what I remember."

Donte rubbed the back of his neck with one hand as
he spoke for the first time. "I remember the mud too,
Mother. Direon and I were with him. You were home
with the twins."

McKenna circled above them, up and down on the
wind, but did not get close enough to touch the trees or
to be seen. Hilda unclenched her hands and approached
her sons, reaching for them as if looking for them to
steady her. Both boys took her and placed her hands on
their shoulders.

"But I do remember," Hilda said, a cry escaping her
lips. "I remember the hogs, the sound of them rooting
just before they caught sight of him. They started, ran
wild, and I screamed just before they knocked him to the
ground and killed him. I recall every detail as if I had
been there, but I remember being home with the babies
too. Darlo had a fever and wouldn't stop crying. Dristan
slept like such a good boy, my quiet boy. How can I have
two memories?"

"The Women," Direon hissed. "The Women have

33

done something to our memories. It must be them. They control all. They have power they shouldn't have over our lives."

McKenna's blood ran cold. She wondered how many times she might have descended and slapped her hand over someone's mouth before the words were spoken. She might have saved some of them. Maybe she could have prevented them becoming subject to the judgment of the Women.

But McKenna always did her job. Without fail, she delivered the fae to their fate. A pall of dread blanketed her, and she felt herself slipping from the wind's grasp and descending just a bit.

Her mind screamed at her to do something, that she could settle the family down and possibly salvage the situation. Just as she started to sink a bit farther, she saw another person slink out of the darkness behind Hilda's boys. She knew before he came into view that it was Maksim. He was a *bogle* faery, and he took his job seriously.

In earlier fae history, a *bogle* would punish young children who disobeyed their parents or torment people who were lazy. Now, the Women used them as their most dedicated Sentinels.

If Maksim had heard Direon's words, then she would have no chance to spare Hilda's sons. They were enemies of the Women now, and in order to protect the secrecy of the rebellion, she had to complete her duty as a Sentinel.

Maksim caught sight of her just before he entered the light. He grinned and McKenna nodded. *Bogles* were ugly fae, with bulbous noses and long arms attached to squatty, beefy torsos. She always attributed their unattractive appearance to the doctrine of *here, it is what is.*

"McKenna," Maksim spoke in a coarse, guttural voice. "Would you like to do the honors or shall I?"

CHAPTER 6

ROBBIE WAS ENTIRELY caught up in the sensa-
tions of flying, closing his eyes and giving his mind
over to the lifting and turning and dropping of his stomach with each shift McKenna made in their aerial ven-
ture. After a while, he opened his eyes only to find that
she had stopped traveling and was now circling above a
spot in the woods.

When he recovered his senses and gazed below
them, he saw three fae, a woman and two men. One of
the males had a torch that bled yellow light across their
group.

His weasel ears worked many times better than his
human ones, so it wasn't hard to detect the words being
exchanged once he'd decided to pay attention.

After just a moment, he recognized them as Hilda
and her sons Direon and Donte. Robbie visited her from

time to time when he passed near her home. She had a particular bush that produced a combination of nuts. When she discovered that he liked the small almonds, she would toss them to him out of her window, insisting she only liked the fat ones.

"...I screamed just before they knocked him to the ground and killed him. I recall every detail as if I had been there, but I remember being home with the babies, too. Darlo had a fever and wouldn't stop crying. Dristan slept like such a good boy, my quiet boy. How can I have two memories?"

Hilda was speaking, and clearly she was emotionally distraught about whatever was happening. Her sons were tending to her, holding her up and caressing her arm when she swayed on her feet. Then one of them mentioned the Women, his tone vitriolic, and Robbie physically detected McKenna's muscles grow taut.

He knew enough about the circumstances in the faery realm to know what the man's words meant. They were treasonous to the Women's steel hold on the faery realm, and it was McKenna's job to spy and catch traitors.

Opening his mouth to ask her what she would do, Robbie stopped short when he noticed a new person entering the scene. He was an ugly man, and the only word that came to mind was "troll." He didn't know whether they had trolls in the faery realm or if they were even fae, but this guy certainly looked like one.

Robbie was still contemplating the ugly man's

species when he spoke to McKenna, revealing their presence just above the tree line. His lovely pilot didn't seem surprised based on the stony look plastered to her face. He could feel a shuddering in her body, and it took a moment to grasp that she was fluttering her wings rapidly so that they could descend slowly.

"I will, Maksim," she told the short troll-man. Then she waved her hand and a golden door opened.

Another man, this one tall and stocky, appeared just inside the doorway. He was so massive that his arms bulged and stuck out on either side of him. His eyebrows were pale and almost invisible, giving the impression that he had red hair though his scalp was shaven.

"What's happening here?" the younger of the sons, Donte, demanded, shielding his mother and backing away from the golden door.

The powerlifter guy stepped across the threshold, glancing from Maksim to McKenna and back again. "Which of you will report it?" he asked.

With wide eyes, Robbie watched the big bald man wave both hands in front of the woman and her two sons. All three of their bodies went slack, though still standing upright. Their eyes glazed over, and it was clear they were all under a hypnotic spell. The man muttered some words in a language Robbie knew was probably Gaelic and then the threesome stepped one by one through the golden door.

Still hovering in the air above them, McKenna tossed the troll an indifferent look, raising an eyebrow up not speaking.

Maksim chuckled. "She called you. She should have the honors."

With a bored sigh, McKenna shook her head to Maksim. "No, I am long from the end of my flight. The honor is yours." She made a sweeping motion with her hand. "It is much easier for you to resume your job than it is for me to rise up on the wind again."

"Ah, beautiful, McKenna. You are too kind." The troll only got uglier when an ear-to-ear grin split his face. "Is that a rat?" He glanced at Robbie before reaching a hand up as if he intended to pet him.

Although his torso was wrapped up tight against McKenna's abdomen, the hairs of his back bristled in a hackle. They were flying too high for the short man to get too close to him, but Robbie opened his mouth and bared his teeth, snarling.

"Whoa... Not a friendly rat either."

Robbie would've liked the chance to draw blood, but just in case he had any ideas of wriggling free and doing so, McKenna flapped her wings and caught the breeze. She sailed high towards the stars like a rocket, making his stomach lurch up into his throat.

He swallowed to keep his supper in place. His mind wandered without his control as his eyes closed, and as it did, the urge to vomit nearly overtook him.

"Mama needs you, darling. You know she needs you. Please do this one thing for Mama."

It was never just one thing. She'd used the same entreaty just a week ago. But he had done her biding. And he would do it again. He would do it because of the way she looked at him. Because of the hollowness in her eyes and the movement of muscle at her jaw as she chewed her tongue in desperate need.

"I know, Mama. I know," he soothed, patting her hand and then kissing her cheek. She sucked in a breath, moaning in pain. He shouldn't have touched her. Shouldn't have gotten so close. He knew she desired him above all others, and when she was blood-starved to this point, it was all she could do to deny herself his blood.

"I'll be back soon. I promise."

Veronica Weir had only been a vampire for about eight years. She had given up all that she'd owned to be changed just eighteen months after Robin's birth. Witchcraft had not been enough for the beautiful woman, and she'd believed that becoming a vampire would assuage her desire for more.

More what, Robin didn't know or understand. At almost ten years of age, he couldn't think of a single reason his mother would want to become a bloodsucker. And more than needing the blood, she wanted magical blood. It was a drug to her, a need that ate at her from the inside out if she didn't get what she needed.

Robin hated what he had to do, but his mother was suffering. And he loved her. When she wasn't in her current state, she doted on him like he was her little prince. He wanted to please her and to help get rid of her pain.

Finding and luring a magical child here for her to suckle from was a small price to pay.

So why then did his stomach twist and turn like he was going to throw up?

CHAPTER 7

THE REST of the night flight was uneventful, and McKenna was grateful that Robbie didn't do much talking. Just before sunset, the winds died off, and she floated down to the ground, planting slippered feet into the grass and bending her knees to absorb any impact. Both hands reached behind her to untie the band holding her passenger, struggling with shaking fingers and tired, tense back muscles before she could get him free.

He tumbled into the dirt, rolling in a little ball before finding his feet and scurrying to the cabin. McKenna followed suit, closing the door behind her and then securing the shutters on the windows as well. The hearth fire was dying, which was just as well, as they had no need of heat or to cook for the moment. Still, she poked at it in quick, sharp movements while Robbie checked the cabin.

When he felt that the coast was clear, she knew he

would shift into his human form, and it was all she could do to keep her eyes on the red-tinged coals. She didn't hear his claws scratching on the floor anymore so she took the chance to glance up. Her eyes skimmed the firm skin of his naked backside just as he was sliding his pants up to cover himself. He turned, giving her a half-smile.

"Rough night, huh?"

A breath she hadn't realized she had been holding rushed from her parted lips, and she dropped her eyes to the dirt floor. "Yes, yes, it was." She looked long and hard at the pallet beside the window then back up at him. "We've sort of disrupted our schedule."

"Yeah, we have." He took a few steps closer, reaching one hand up across his chest to massage the opposite shoulder. "But then the faery assembly yesterday already had us in disarray."

"Yes."

"McKenna…"

His green eyes were boring into her, seeking her soul. Utter exhaustion left her limbs tingling, heavy, and weak. More than that, her brain was tired. She didn't want to expend the energy it took to keep up her guard with Robin, as she usually did.

As if sensing her vulnerability, he swooped close to her in long strides. He was several inches taller than she, and his breaths came fast and hot against her face. She refused to look up at him, instead fixing her eyes on his chest. But then that too was a mistake because he was a glorious-looking man, sculpted like an Adonis but with a sprinkling of dark hair along the valley of his breast-bone.

"I can't think with you standing there," she spoke, disliking the desperate twinge in her words.

"McKenna..." he said again, leaning forward to place a kiss to her forehead. He didn't pull back, his lips lingering against her skin as he continued speaking. "You do too much thinking as it is. Let go. For once in your life, just let go."

"I can't." A tremor shimmied down her spine. "If I do, I don't think I'll be able to pick myself back up again."

His hands touched both hips, sliding around her backside to firmly tug her against him. "That's what I'm here for. I'll help you pick yourself back up...after I've laid you flat on your back."

Her head fell forward to touch his chest, sliding to the side so that she could rub her cheek against the firmness of his body. Her eyes were closed, but she could feel his torso twisting, and before she could think, his lips found hers, a single finger at her chin tipping her face up closer to his.

It was hard to remember the last time she'd been kissed. It must have been in her youth, when things were open and innocent and possible. Before the beckoning of the Women. Before she had discovered the truth of her world's existence. Before she had first played a role in turning over her people to be stripped of all that they were.

Yes, it must have been before all of that, when she

was just a woman wanting to be loved.

A sob rose up into her throat, but the mere thought of letting one shred of darkness invade this moment made her angry. In reaction, she dug her nails into Robin's back as if squeezing away any sadness from her being.

Robin made a sound like a growl and scooped her back into his arms as he dropped to his knees on the pallet. His kiss to her lips turned hard and insistent in sharp contrast to the tenderness of his hands settling her onto the makeshift bed.

"You can go back to being cold and aloof with me tomorrow, but now, in this moment, I'm going to make you hot."

She was already hot, and that was an understatement. His mouth was working its way along her neck and collarbone, but her lips were swollen and bruised from his kisses. Her tongue darted out to lick her heated lips. Then she leaned up to kiss the lobe of his ear.

Robin ground his body into her with a rough sigh, his hand pulling her loose tunic top away from her shoulder. The material ripped open, but she ceased to care when one of her nipples was swallowed into his mouth. He teased the bud with his teeth, and McKenna practically leapt off the pallet in rapture.

"Robin, please." She had no idea what she was pleading for. More of the same treatment to that wing or perhaps equal to the other. Or maybe she was begging for something else entirely.

Her gossamer wings quivered, moving of their own accord and tickling against her naked back. Robin reached a hand out to touch one of them, skimming his fingers in a feather-soft stroke along the outside edge. A rush of pleasure sailed through her limbs and her eyes rolled into the back of her head. A faery's wings, though delicate, were also one of the most sensitive areas of the body. Her reaction to the caress surged red hot to her center.

When Robin's hand cupped her between the thighs, the pressure ignited that spark of desire straight into her. and she whimpered for more. He found her lips again, crushing them in a deep kiss while both hands worked her leggings down her hips. When the cotton material reached her ankles, McKenna kicked them away before she tugged at Robin's shoulders, trying to bring him between her legs.

It wasn't what she was searching for because she wanted him, the man, but Robin's fingers delved into the blonde curls between her legs, two of them gliding easily into her wet heat. Her body reacted instantly, hips thrusting to meet each movement of his hand.

He worked her easily, building the tension inside her, forcing her breath to catch in her throat. When he added his thumb to the mix, flicking it against that most sensitive spot, she cried out, "Ohhhhh…"

"You're beautiful like this," he told her, gazing down at her with sex-heavy eyes. "I knew you'd be this beautiful if I could just get you to let down your guards."

McKenna wasn't a complete innocent, having had her share of lovers in the past. Still, Robin was as skilled as any man she'd ever known, and she could feel that he would have her tipping over the edge into a climax within moments.

"Robin, come to me," she gasped, rolling her head back and forth as he continued thrusting and touching her. "Please don't let me go alone."

His hands left her so quickly that she felt at once naked and hollow, the ache inside her screaming to be fulfilled. Her eyes flitted open and she watched him remove the very pants he'd only put on a few moments ago. He knelt there a moment, looking at her while his erection bobbed proudly in front of her. She reached out to clasp it with a trembling hand. The sound of his guttural moan gave her a sense of power as she sought to find control again.

"No, McKenna," Robin murmured, brushing her hand away and dropping down to smother her body with his. "You're not the one calling these shots. You're mine right now."

One hand reached up to her jaw, clasping her face roughly. She opened her mouth and he forced his thumb between her teeth, pressing her head to the side even as he drove himself so deep into her that she thought he must have pierced her very core. His dominance thrilled her, awakening her senses in a way she'd never experienced. She wanted this. She needed it. Her mind, body, and soul had to be taken hard and fast and rough.

It was all she could do to reach up and wrap her arms around him, biting his thumb and moaning in exquisite pleasure as he pounded in and out of her.

"Yes," he growled, nipping at her shoulder. "Mine. You're fucking mine."

He grabbed her backside, lifting her hips to meet his movements, and she mewled when he plunged even deeper. The tension, the heat, the friction all took over every nerve in her body. The pressure built until everything sparked into a brilliant flash of light before her eyes. McKenna screamed, the sound reverberating off of the rafters, before Robin's hand forcefully covered her mouth with his in a kiss that stole her breath.

Even as her limbs fell loose after her release, Robin's body tensed and he drove hard one last time as he growled her name against her ear.

CHAPTER 8

ROBIN AWOKE on his side, his arms circling the most alluring body he could ever remember holding. When he took a deep breath, a mouthful of hair got sucked between his lips, and he inhaled the scent of her a moment before blowing it out of his mouth. McKenna wriggled in his arms, sighing in contentment.

A glance at the window above them showed a sliver of light, though not very bright. His body told him even without clear evidence that it was just a few hours before sunset. He wasn't sure why, but somehow he had retained some of his animal instincts even when in human form. He could oftentimes sense other people or animals approaching the cabin, and his internal clock was rarely incorrect about time.

With a deep breath, he leaned up on one elbow before he began combing back McKenna's hair from her temple. She swallowed, still sleeping, and curled into his caress.

It was a shame to wake her as he knew she hadn't had a good sleep in days. Her expression was soft, not a wrinkle of worry marring an inch on her golden face. Still, he couldn't let her miss her night flight. There were still many things he didn't know about this world, but he wasn't about to allow McKenna to fall into disfavor with the Women. Banishment or loss of magic were things he knew about, and those were things he would never want to see happen to her.

"Hey, you," he whispered close to her ear, kissing and then taking the lobe between his teeth. "Time to wake up. Aren't you hungry?"

As if in response, his own stomach growled. With a start, McKenna opened her eyes and scrambled to sit upright. Noticing her nakedness, she clasped the blanket up to her chin, wings aflutter, and looked down at Robin, who was still lying naked beside her. A kaleidoscope of emotions passed across her face, displaying an array of different thoughts crossing her mind.

Robin chuckled and leaned up to kiss her forehead. "I like whatever made you blush the best."

"What?" she demanded, snatching the covers closer when he tried to kiss her lips.

"Whatever thought you were just having that made you blush. That's the one I like best. Feel free to blush again."

She did, but this time she paired it with a frown so

intense that a little indentation developed between her eyebrows.

"Fine." Robin stood and slipped on his pants before he headed for the kitchen area. "Go back to the ice queen. I'm going to rustle up some food because having sex with you has made me very hungry."

The sound he heard her make could have been a groan or a whine or both. Regardless, it caused him to smile. He knew he was in for the same old treatment from her again. That was okay. He would recover his place as her lackey for the moment. But both of them knew now that he could reduce her icy exterior to liquid heat if he wanted.

For now, it was enough just to know it.

There was still a good amount of cheese and sausage left over from Gavin and his wife, so he set out another buffet of items for them to enjoy. He preferred to hunt in the daytime, but they hadn't had meat for a hot meal in some time. So as he worked, slicing up cheese, he decided he'd go out tonight.

"I'll try to rustle up a rabbit tonight. Or maybe a pheasant."

McKenna didn't respond. When he looked, he saw that she had her back to him as she slipped into a clean pair of leggings and a tunic. Her top had slits in the back to allow her wings to slip through. They glistened with an aurora of color. He'd studied those wings just before they'd both gone to sleep. To his amazement, they weren't so fragile as the wings of a dragonfly, which is what they resembled. They were thicker than he would have imagined, though still mostly translucent. He wanted to ask her about them, curious as to the biology.

Judging by her tense shoulders and stern expression, she wouldn't be open to that sort of small talk at the moment.

After she'd finished dressing, she turned to him and gave him a long hard look. "Of course, if you'd like. To go hunting, I mean. I know I haven't made anything fresh in some time. It's lucky we haven't had any visitors."

Most *sylphe* faeries considered their homes available for night travelers, since they rarely occupied their homes in the dark hours. As such, it was McKenna's custom to have something warming in the hearth for anyone who would stop by. When Robin discovered his ability to shift into human form, they installed small latches on the insides of the doors and windows so that he could at least have forewarning to shift back into a weasel if anyone did show.

McKenna left the cabin after they'd eaten, and Robin locked the door after her so that he could clean up following their meal. When the cabin was as it should be, he unlocked the door and then stripped off his pants in order to shift into a weasel again.

As he dashed out into the night, his thoughts turned to McKenna. Even with the silent treatment from her, he was still in a good mood. Considering his circumstances the day he had crossed that threshold from the human realm, he decided he couldn't complain one bit about where he was now. His time in the faery realm had started out frightening, but when McKenna took him in, he'd found someone willing to give him a second chance.

He had still been nothing more than a talking weasel in those early days, and part of him had known that the beautiful blonde woman thought of him more as a pet. A useful pet, but one nonetheless. She had chatted with him while she rubbed his furry head, allowed him to minister to her the same way a person might accept the licking and nuzzling of a favored dog.

But in that time, Robbie's affection for her had grown. Perhaps it was some weird psychological attachment, but he had known months ago that he was developing feelings for her. When he had learned to transform back into a man, he'd hoped she might want some further intimacy between them.

McKenna was a professional at keeping her feelings closely guarded. She had no choice under the circumstances. Last night was a perfect example. Only because he knew her so well had he realized the horror underlying her aloof exterior when the old lady and her two boys had been caught questioning the Women's governance.

Robbie was so intent on his thoughts that he almost didn't recognize the sound of footsteps. He halted and cocked his head to listen, standing up onto his back feet so that he could see farther off through the forest. He recognized the red-haired faery and his dark companion even though they were many yards away.

"'Lo!" he called to them, scampering through the

brush to meet up with them.

"Hey, there," Rooney smiled as Robbie crawled up his body to perch on his shoulder. "We were just coming to see you."

A sense of foreboding settled in Robbie's belly, but he scratched at his whiskered face and grinned. "Got some goodies for us?"

Roon's lover Belle was from the human world, and she had crossed over, along with three children, to escape Lodar's clutches. As the surrogate mom to those kids, she also made some of the best cookies he'd ever tasted. She had taken to bringing him some every so often.

The beautiful raven-haired Siren held up a basket with a smile, indicating that she did indeed have some goodies for him. Still, the worry in his gut persisted. Coming at night—and without the children—was unusual.

The three of them headed off towards the cabin, and Robbie found himself glancing left and right in nervousness. He wondered if there might be Sentinels watching them and whether their meeting would raise the ire of anyone who did see them.

"So where are the kids?"

"Oh." Rooney grinned and tugged Belle close, nuzzling her neck. "Mom thought we should have some alone time for some reason."

He watched Belle roll her eyes and shove him away. "The truth is that Rooney's mother misses her chicks and so she'll use any excuse to get ours under her roof."

Even though the two girls and one boy weren't really Belle's biological children, she and Roon were raising them as their own. The situation seemed to be working out well, although Roon and his father had to add on a few extra rooms to his small cabin to accommodate the sudden burgeoning family.

When they got back to McKenna's cabin, Robbie did a quick search for Sentinels before ushering his guests to the table. "Okay, so what's going on?"

Belle dropped her head back and began to hum low in her throat. Anyone else might assume she was a loon, but Robbie knew about her abilities. She was a Siren, one of the extinct race of fae who could manipulate sound. Her humming was a way of creating a protective cocoon around them so that no one lurking outside could hear their conversation.

"Fómhar contacted Belle yesterday."

"The Autumn Woman?"

Rooney's normally gregarious face was pinched in seriousness. "Yes. She had a message. We got here as soon as we could."

"A message for me? Why the hell would she have a message for me?"

The other man shook his red head, leaning forward and tapping his finger on the table. "Not you specifically. For the rebels."

"Holy fuck. She knows about the Dissenters? *They* know about the Dissenters?"

Belle broke her humming and looked at Robbie with

intense black eyes. "She doesn't know. Not specifically. She just thinks there are 'pockets of fae contemplating rebellion.'" Then she began droning again, head back.

"What was the message?"

"She said the Women can no longer contain Báisteach. She's stronger than they are and she plans... she plans to destroy the Island Anethemusa."

Robbie let that sink in a moment. He had been McKenna's contact with the island inhabitants almost since the day she had convinced him to ally with her. The people on Anethemusa were outcasts, stripped of their powers and left to fend for themselves without assistance from the Women. Drought, flood, blizzards, hurricane-like storms—they were susceptible to all of those without the Women to maintain the climate. McKenna's aunt was also one of those on that island.

"When?" he whispered, his stomach lurching.

"Belle isn't sure. Soon."

Robbie scrunched up his furry brow. "Wait a minute. How did one of the Women talk to Belle? Did she just come down off that hill and track her down? Wouldn't Báisteach know she talked to Belle?"

Belle spoke again. "The vibrations. Through the trees in the Autumn." Then she resumed the sounds.

"She's been learning her powers," Rooney explained. "She can feel things and can read things from the nature here. We were bringing the children to my parents' house in the Autumn and Belle felt a tree calling to her. It was Fómhar, speaking through the life forces of the tree."

"Soon," Robbie muttered, using his paws to scratch at his chest. "Soon."

Rooney and Belle made to leave, but before opening the door, the faery turned to look down at Robbie with a strange glint in his eye. In one sudden movement, he stooped down and took the weasel by the scruff of his neck, holding him up helpless in front of his face.

"I know what you did, Robbie. To Devvie. I know what you were. If you betray us, if you do anything to hurt my people, I'll string your ass up by your tail and feed you to the fae piranhas. It will take those razor-toothed fish weeks to pick the last bit of meat from your bones."

CHAPTER 9

FLITTING AROUND in a small circle, McKenna studied the cottage below her with a heavy heart. It was clear by the darkness and quiet that Hilda was not there. The hour was early morning, and she knew the older woman should be home, a fire going in her hearth. Even though this was the Summer, it was forever chilly overnight, so most fae homes had smoke wafting from their chimneys.

McKenna shouldn't have expected her to be there. Direon's and Donte's homes were also cold and silent. McKenna knew the drill. They weren't coming back.

Maksim would have accompanied Hilda and her boys to the Women. He would have regurgitated what he'd heard, and if the Women believed them a threat, they would have handed down punishment.

The infraction was so small, she thought. *Nothing*

more than chatter and rumor.

But McKenna knew that Maksim would have embellished the details. He was a nasty man and got a sick pleasure from watching people suffer. Also, he received high recompense for his service. Value in the fae world was measured in barters. Maksim used his position as a Sentinel to manipulate other faeries so that he could receive more than his fair share of produce and services and foodstuffs.

The Women were well aware of his behavior. They just chose to turn a blind eye in order to keep one of their top Sentinels at their beck and call.

McKenna forced her thoughts from Hilda and her boys, sweeping west of the darkened cabin with a heavy sigh. She told herself that it did no good to obsess over it because it would only feed the bitterness, which she couldn't afford now.

Of course, avoiding the one topic left room for thoughts on the other topic she wanted to avoid.

Robin.

She couldn't believe she'd been so foolish as to let down her guard with him. Kissing him was bad enough, but falling into bed… her cheeks flamed as she remembered how good it felt when his hands grabbed her, holding her down and giving her no choice but to submit.

Oh, it had felt good to let go and allow him to take her. Her life was like a tightly sealed box. Holding on to each emotion, controlling all her reactions at every turn was exhausting and strained her in ways she sometimes didn't even realize.

But in Robin's arms, all that tension had evaporated. He had smothered away all her cognizance of the rebellion, leaving her with only raw, aching need. Need that he'd quickly fulfilled to her greatest imagining.

The memory made her ache for him. Heat coiled between her legs and her nipples tightened with desire. This was no good. She couldn't let herself lose control again. Love was a dangerous prospect that would leave her vulnerable. Being vulnerable put the Dissenters at risk.

More than that, she knew the type of person Robin had been in his human life. She trusted him with knowledge of the rebellion, but she couldn't trust him with her heart.

"Damn!" She cursed herself and her waxing thoughts.

She continued her flight, only halfheartedly monitoring the goings-on in her sector. When the shimmery pink light of sunrise made its appearance on the horizon, she breathed a sigh of relief that her night was over. She hoped that sleep would help her put a better hold on her emotions.

The wind dropped McKenna gently to the dirt a few feet from her cabin. She shook her head and brushed her blonde hair from her face, rubbing her eyes with the heels of her hand. Exhaustion made her legs heavy and clumsy as she stumbled towards the door.

"You look like something the cat dragged in."

To her credit, McKenna didn't gasp or start or show

any sign of surprise, though inside she trembled. Turning with slow intent, she faced Maksim with a raised eyebrow and a bored gaze. "Something I can help you with?"

"Shift's over, huh, and it seems it was a pretty quiet night for you. You losing your touch or just your eyesight?"

"You are an annoying little man." She knew that would get his dander up. He hated being reminded of how small he was, especially given how large his aspirations were.

"Don't you like your job, McKenna? I know I do." His face twisted with a demented smile as he approached her. "I mean, there is the thrill of it. There is the skill it takes to catch just that slightest movement or tick that signals that someone is up to something. I get a charge when I find one of their soft underbellies. And they're always surprised."

She raised her head a bit so that she could look down at him, staring at him with a cold, hard glare.

"Sometimes they're surprised because they don't even know they've done something wrong. The poor oblivious fools. But sometimes"—he was toe-to-toe with her now, one chubby finger reached out to graze the hem of her long tunic—"sometimes they're surprised because they think they've been so clever and that no one could possibly know their secrets. Those are the best ones."

"Why are you telling me this? If you've got someone to turn over, then do it. You don't need me in the first place, and in the second, my shift is over. I'm going to sleep." She turned on her heel, tossing her hair across her shoulder.

"Does that human keep your bed warm for you when you're flying about?"

She stopped with her hand at the door, swallowing down bile and feeling it burn in her chest. Still, she managed to issue an exasperated snort as she placed her hand on the door to step inside. "Yes, Maksim. The little weasel keeps a spot on my pillow warm for me. Now get out of here and let me get to bed."

She could hear him chuckling as she entered her cabin, but the sound was getting softer so she knew he was doing as she'd said and was leaving her property. When she was safely inside, her body sagged against the closed door and she raised a shaky hand to her forehead.

The strong, hot hands that grabbed her—one at her waist to haul her to him and the other at her neck to lift her lips to his—were the most comforting touch she could have imagined. All previous thoughts of maintaining distance from Robin were gone. She needed him, thirsted for him, had to have him again.

McKenna opened her mouth and plunged her tongue into his, seeking to taste as much of him as she could. His fingers dug into her skin, demanding more, and in answer, she nipped at his lip with her teeth.

She was more than surprised when he pulled away, backing into the table with a growl.

"We need to talk."

CHAPTER 10

"OKAY," MCKENNA PANTED. "If talk is what you want, then talk."

The woman had Robin in knots. His cock was throbbing to be buried deep inside her, and he knew good and well if he crossed that room and slipped his hands into her leggings that he would find her wet and ready for him. Still, he could see the ice leeching into her gaze again, her natural defense to deny all emotion.

The temptation to grab her and throw her down on the pallet was almost too much to fight, but he was unwilling to give into his baser needs. Even so, Robin didn't want to see her freeze up completely again either.

"Don't go all frigid on me, McKenna. You damned sure know that f I wanted to I could fuck the hell out of you right now and you wouldn't put up a single word of argument."

A glowing green light flickered from the palm of McKenna's hand and her eyes flashed anger as she stomped to the table. She smacked her hand down and the energy exploded from between her fingers before dissipating into little puffs of smoke.

"Dammit, Robin! This isn't a game. What happened was a mistake and I won't make it again. I have a mission to complete and I can't do it in your arms."

Robin circled around the table in no more than three strides, capturing her lips with his. Her taut muscles went slack as her body molded to his, her surrender immediate. And it wasn't hard to make the decision to plunder her body once he had her in his arms again. Without breaking contact with her mouth, he reached down and yanked her pants down.

McKenna moaned when he tore his lips from hers and then gasped when he turned her and forced her back onto the table. He could see the look in her eyes signaling that she was looking for a reason to stop whatever he had in mind.

And he had no intention of allowing that. With a slow, fluid movement, he slipped her leggings off completely, her slippers dropping to the floor with them. At the same time, he placed his palm to her breastbone and pushed her onto her back. The intensity in his eyes said there would be no room for argument.

Just to make sure of that, he took hold of her wrists in one hand, holding them above her head. He palmed her breast with his free hand for just a moment, only long enough draw forth a sharp intake of breath. Then he ventured lower. His fingers easily pressed between her wet folds, entering her in a slow, smooth movement. The feeling of her muscles tightening around him made his body jerk with need.

When he knew she wouldn't fight him, he released her hands and settled on his knees between her legs. Leaning forward, he flicked his tongue across her wet, womanly bits, and she bucked off the table with a cry of mingled protest and pleasure. He licked her up and down slowly. The taste of her was exquisite, and he found himself intoxicated by the act of pleasuring her. She mewled and moaned, and he reached up with both hands to grasp her inner thighs and open her even wider for him. She tensed, grinding her hips to his mouth. Within just a few moments, she exploded with release.

After easing her down from her climax, Robin rose so that he could drop his head against her breast. He listened to the thudding of her heart in her chest and then smiled when her arms reached up to clutch him closer in an embrace.

"Thank you," she breathed, combing the hair at his temple.

It was a silly thing to say. He wanted to thank her for giving herself over to him, for allowing him the honor of making love to her. And that was when it occurred to him that this was the first time he had ever truly made love to a woman.

Certainly it the first time he'd ever given himself

over solely to the act of pleasuring his partner without any expectation of reciprocation. He was still achingly hard for her, but he knew in that moment that he would be perfectly content to just hold her. It would be enough to stay exactly this way for a long, long time.

"You said we needed to talk."

With a deep sigh, Robin nodded. He turned his head into her breast, inhaling her scent, then tilted up to kiss her chin. Propping his head on his elbow, he looked down at her, taking in the lovely flush of her cheeks and the beautiful warmth in her green eyes.

"Rooney and Belle were here last night."

If not for his body so closely knit to hers, he wouldn't have known the anxiety that coiled up inside her. "They saw you, didn't they? They know you can shift into a human."

He shook his head. "No, they didn't see me. You know I'm careful. Why would you say that?"

"Maksim knows. He stopped me outside just as I returned from my flight. He made a suggestion about you warming my bed. Somehow he knows."

Robin pursed his lips and gazed at a spot just above her head. He considered the ugly little faery he'd seen a few nights earlier. He couldn't imagine how the creep had discovered Robin's secret. "What does that mean? Is it a crime for me to shift from weasel to human?"

"It's a crime for me to keep secrets from the Women. I am a Sentinel and it's my job to notify them of anything unusual. You crossed over into our world, and you should not have the power to shift. Keeping that from them was for my own gain so that I could continue to use you as my messenger."

He flicked his eyes back to hers, cocking the side of his lips up in a grin. "I'm not just your messenger anymore. Don't forget that." Pausing, he looked into her eyes, searching for some sign of agreement. She said nothing, but the warmth in her gaze was at least not a disagreement. "So what happens? Will he report us to the Women?"

He was more than a little pleased when she raised her head and pecked his lips. "I don't know. He should have reported us already. But he's a conniving man and there's no telling what he's really up to."

Robin's voice lowered and his brows pursed together. "What happened to Hilda and her sons?"

CHAPTER 11

MCKENNA'S BREATH SHUDDERED from her lips, and she dropped her head back onto the table with a thud. "They weren't at their homes"

"Which means what?"

She closed her eyes and rolled her head back and forth, almost as if she could deny the truth of things. "Whatever Maksim told the Women was clearly sufficient to dole out punishment. I hope"—she swallowed—"that they are on the island Anethemusa."

He rolled off of her and stood with an angry shake of his fists. "For speaking against the Women? What they said was so small, so minor. They would be stripped of all their powers and banished to the island? How do your people stand for this?"

McKenna stood and wiggled into her leggings before answering. She had to crawl under the table to find one of her discarded slippers, and once she was dressed again, she rounded the table to keep herself from his grasp again. She needed a clear head if they were going to have a discussion and not end up in each other's arms again.

"Most of the people don't know, because of the wishes." She saw the way Robin's face scrunched up in consternation and knew he still didn't understand. "Fae are given two wishes. They usually use the first one up in their youth. The second is saved for the time of death. Most of us would use that wish to assuage our family's anguish when we die. The banished fae are urged to use their wishes…to make their families forget."

"Urged? As in forced?"

"Yes," she whispered. "Upon threat that their families will be next."

He was silent for several minutes, but the boiling emotion under the surface was clear in the way that his chest rose and fell with long gulps of air. "You know, it's really ironic. I thought this place was different. I mean, from almost the moment I got here, I knew about your rebellion, but I still fooled myself into thinking it was different. But something tells me now that life will be the same no matter where I go."

The glint in his eyes scared her. It was primal and angry and so intense that it made her hair stand on end. Her mind reacted, yearning to join him, to be and feel and breathe anger.

She couldn't give in completely, but under careful

restraint she spoke, her voice low, gruff, and serious. "It may be that someday they will take the wrong fae up to that hill. Maybe one day it will all be a trap and it will be the end of their reign. It's the Women, Robin. They are the root of this. They have to be stopped. They will be stopped."

"They know about the rebellion, McKenna. That's what Roon and Belle came to tell us."

The blood drained from her face and a chill crawled along her arms. She shivered, crossing her hands to clasp her own elbows in an embrace. "It's over, then? It's over before it's begun?"

"No." He rounded the table with arms outstretched to her, but she backed away with a warning scowl. Robin dropped his hands in resignation, rubbing the palms on his hips as her spoke again. "Belle said Fómhar spoke to her and told her to get a message to the rebellion. Báisteach is out of control and even the other Women can't restrain her."

McKenna's mind buzzed, drowning in a sea of dizzying thoughts. She hugged herself tighter, swallowing past a huge lump in her throat. "What is the message?"

"She's going to destroy Anethemusa. They're not sure when, but she means to do it and her sisters cannot stop her."

"If they can't stop her, then what good is it to tell us? The Women are powerful—the most powerful beings in the faery realm. If they're saying they can't control one of their own, then what the hell good is any of it? There's nothing to do."

His crestfallen expression was more than she could take. She closed her eyes so that she wouldn't have to see it, wouldn't have to be pierced by the disappointment in those green eyes of his. It was just a shadow of the disappointment she knew she would see in Aoi's eyes if she had been before her at that moment. She knew she would see it in any of the islanders' eyes. In any of the Dissenters' eyes.

"You don't get to give up. Not now. There's always a way, McKenna. You believe in this, in your cause. Don't betray it."

"What do you care, Robin?" She looked at him through burning tears that she refused to let fall. "This isn't your fight. If I betray the rebellion, it changes nothing for you. Even if I'm not here, you've only lost a roof over your head. And with that sexy smile and those eyes, I'm sure you will find another's roof to shelter under soon enough."

Her hands rose up in a protective stance again, waving him back when he approached her. But this time he wouldn't be put off. He scooped her up with tender arms. It was so opposite the other times he took her in his arms with strong, rough hands. His caress was no less effective as a feather-soft touch. She melted into his embrace, dropping her head back to look up at him.

"I don't give a fuck about this rebellion, McKenna. It's you I care about. The cause is a part of you. And I refuse to let you betray yourself. The woman I found in here?" His palm pressed flat to her breast, splaying wide over her heart. "This woman is what I can't afford to lose to this fight."

"What should I do?" she begged, her voice so soft she almost couldn't even hear it herself. Her eyes rolled back and closed when he brushed her hair back at her temple and cradled her closer.

"Sleep. You should sleep now. When you're rested, we'll figure this out."

"We will?" Eyes still closed, she allowed him to lead her to the bed pallet.

"Well, mostly you will. But I'll follow right along for the ride."

Robin started to rise after he had her tucked into the blankets, but McKenna clutched his hand with a ragged breath. "Stay with me. Lie with me."

His green eyes narrowed as he studied her and she wondered at his hesitation. He'd forced his touch upon her these last several days, but now he stopped a moment. The corners of his lips upturned in a small smile. "I needed you to ask me. I'm not sure why, but I needed it today," he confessed. Then he lifted the covers, slipped in beside her, and tugged her against his front so that they could spoon.

McKenna's eyes drifted shut, and feeling safe, she fell into sleep instantly.

$\mathcal{C}$HAPTER 12

IT HAD BEEN too long since they'd had any meat for a hot meal, so when McKenna was good and asleep, Robin shifted back to a weasel and went hunting. As a human, he'd never given much thought to weasels. Now that he was one—at least part of the time—it amazed him that he could track down and then kill animals as big as or bigger than himself.

This afternoon he was bringing home one of McKenna's favorites—a chicken. The first time he had brought home a wild fae chicken, McKenna had gone back for seconds and thirds, something she rarely did. He'd commented on it of course, but she'd coyly noted that she was simply hungry. The memory of that, though early in their relationship, was a sweet one for him to recall.

Teeth buried in its neck, Robbie dragged the dead

bird to the cabin and to the door. Normally McKenna would de-feather the bird out in the yard behind the cabin, but when he went inside he glanced at the pallet to find her still asleep. He took a moment to look at her, curled up into a ball, contentment smoothing the lines on her face, then he scurried outside to retrieve the chicken, careful not to get blood on the floor.

"So it falls to me then," he murmured to himself, latching the door and checking the window before shifting into human form so that he could prep the chicken for the spit. As he worked silently over the sink, his mind wandered to long-gone days. These were the memories he longed to forget.

Her eyes were full of tears, wide and wet and glistening. The tears made him feel sad, heartbroken really. But beneath the tears was hunger. It was a hunger he'd seen in her eyes many times before, but now it was tenfold. She reached a finger, trailed it up through the blood he felt dripping down his neck. When she put the red-tipped digit to her lips and tasted it, her eyes, those big brown eyes, rolled back into her head and she moaned in ecstasy.

Robbie was afraid he was going to be sick. The vomit seared its way up his esophagus, and though he clenched his jaw tight and swallowed, it would not be held at bay. With a moan and a heave, he leaned away from her and spilled up his cheeseburger and strawberry milkshake.

The vampire laughed. His heavy palm slapped him on the back as he guffawed. Robbie choked, spewing nasty, vile stuff onto the floor. The hand egging him on like a teenager was the same one that had held his hands behind his back while he ripped and tore and sucked from Robbie's neck.

"This is your boy then?" the vampire chuckled. "He's a bit old for child supplicant, but his blood is bursting with energy. Besides that, he's quite pretty, with those jade eyes and that curling hair. I'll keep him, me-thinks. Give him to me and I'll put you on the list. The next round of magical children will be here before the week's out."

Robbie's mother darted her gaze from the vampire to Robbie and back, over and over. She looked like a caged animal. An animal that saw a way out of its trap.

He knew it had been more than two weeks since she'd had a child to suckle. That was why he was here, giving himself over to this disgusting vampire. The Org dealt in magical children. If Robbie could get a job with them, he was sure he could salvage what little was left of his mother's sanity. Her sanity and her life.

Dizziness overcame him, and he fumbled for the chair beside him to steady himself. The vampire hadn't taken too much from him, but he'd refused to use the rev-erie, and the pain of torn flesh and sinew was almost more than Robbie could take.

"You will provide for him? Schooling, fine clothes, a chance to advance?"

His mother's voice sounded hollow, foreign, and void of any emotion. Even so, she wept. Robbie refused to care. He was bleeding, his neck throbbing and aching with pain, and she spoke of school and luxury.

"He'll become my progeny. He'll make a fine operative one day. And until then, he will serve what purpose he can." The vampire's hand slipped down to Robbie's backside, patting him as a child but with disgusting depravity.

Veronica's cold fingers touched his chin, turning him to look at her. She gently wiped the saliva and vomit from his face then smiled at him. "Finally. It's what we've waited for. We'll never want for anything again."

Robbie's gaze dug into hers, searching. When he didn't find what he was looking for, his eyes dropped to the floor with a resigned exhale. Perhaps Veronica wouldn't want for anything again, but he knew he would. He would want for a mother. A mother he had never had.

"Robin."

A hand touched his shoulder and he instinctively jerked away from it, lost totally to his remembrances. When he looked and saw McKenna's concerned eyes, he shook his head to disrupt the cobwebs. He forced a smile through a shaky breath.

"Get some sleep?"

She offered him a tremulous smile. "I did. Too much probably. That smells delicious." She motioned to the chicken over the fire. "That was what I was saying a moment ago. You were pretty caught up in your own thoughts though."

His head bobbed up and down, but he couldn't trust himself to speak. Silence grew between them until McKenna took a step for the kitchen. He watched her move, admiring the sway of her backside and the flutter of her wings beneath her sweater.

She tore a hunk of bread from the remaining loaf and carried it to the table. He checked the bird and, finding it was cooked through, transferred it to a wooden plate.

He was just placing a huge bite of the piping-hot chicken into his mouth when McKenna spoke. "I want you to warn Aoi and the others. Tell them exactly what Belle said. Explain what Fómhar said. And then get back here. Don't linger."

"So I warn them. What happens then?" He chewed with long, slow movements. There were tiny drummers pounding either side of his head at the temples and he flinched as the act of eating made the pain all the more potent. He figured the thoughts of his past were the cause for his sudden headache and heated cheeks.

"Aoi will tell you what she wants. It's her call whether we begin the revolt, but she'll provide instruction for me through you. But if she gives instructions, if she has some duty for you, come back here first. Before you do anything, I need to know what's going on. Do you understand?"

He turned one corner of his lips up in a knowing

grin, ignoring the discomfort in his brain, then wiped at the grease on his lips with a cotton cloth. "McKenna, are you worried about me?"

CHAPTER 13

MCKENNA WAS WORRIED. Her night flight was over, and she'd returned home to a cold, quiet cabin. Her pallet was smooth and made, indicating that Robin hadn't slept on it. They had left together that evening, her for her Sentinel shift and him for his sojourn to the Island Anethemusa.

"Where the hell is he?" she hissed to herself, slipping into her sweater to warm her wings. She surveyed the empty room and then tamped her foot on the cabin's dirt floor in a pout.

She lifted the same foot and let her slipper drop to the floor before repeating the process with the other. Exhaling a long huff of breath, she dropped down between the blankets of her pallet and closed her eyes to rest. After a few moments, she realized that all her muscles were taut with worry. She clenched her hands then shook them out, trying to release her angst. It didn't take her long to face the fact that she wasn't going to sleep.

Aoi had been more than patient about biding her time to start the rebellion. Even when some of the fae had insisted they wanted to act, Aoi had held them at bay. She insisted that the right moment would arrive and that, when the Dissenters did take up their weapons against the Women, then and only then would they prevail. She was strong-headed and bold enough to make the fae listen.

And the fact that Aoi was a force to be reckoned with was what had McKenna worried. If her aunt decided it was time for action, she might have pressed Robin to do something without coming back to tell McKenna. Robin was part weasel and part man, but otherwise he was defenseless in the faery realm.

Flinging the covers away, McKenna knelt and then stood, dropping her feet into her shoes as she made her way to the door. The sun was low on the horizon, burning a blinding light at the door of the cabin when she stepped out into the yard. Her eyes watered against the brightness, and she took a moment for them to adjust before trudging off into the woods.

"Looking for this?" Maksim stepped from behind a tree, the body of a weasel hanging limp in his outstretched palm.

She was too tired to maintain composure this time. She gasped, a hand reaching up for her open mouth before she could stop herself. Maksim's eyes narrowed in glee. He shook his hand up and down, Robbie's front and back swaying lifelessly with the movement.

"What did you do to him?"

The *bogle* faery chuckled, rearing back so that he could toss the weasel at her feet. "I didn't do anything to your little pet. I found him in the Autumn believe it or not. He was just lying in the dirt like that. He's a little wet, as if he's been in the river or something. Do weasels swim?"

McKenna reached down to pick him up, her stomach tightening with panic but then easing a bit when he opened his eyes to look at her. She could feel Maksim watching her, just waiting for her to give something more away. With an air of indifference, she tossed Robin over her shoulder, trying not to be too rough about it.

"Don't you have somewhere to be, Maksim?"

The faery laughed again, the twinkle in his eye a clear indication that he was enjoying himself. "Yes, I suppose I do. Better get your rat indoors or you'll be looking for another pet to warm your bed for you."

Maksim sauntered away, whistling some unknown tune to himself. She kept her eye on him, watching for him to get out of sight. Then she reached up a hand and stroked Robbie's coat.

"I can't hold this form much longer, McKenna. You've gotta get me to the cabin so I can return to normal."

She wasn't sure what he meant by that, because weasel was his normal form. She barely made it through the door before she felt his body start to warm up, and when she looked, the light inside him started to flicker. She gently placed him on the pallet just as his weasel form burgeoned into that of a human.

"Robin, what did he do to you?" But when she placed her palm to his forehead to brush back his hair, she felt the intense heat of fever sear her fingers. He was sick, terribly sick.

She wasn't sure what to do. Fae never got sick. At least almost never.

He moaned, twisting his neck and jerking his knees up to his chest as if in pain. Pulling the covers up over his naked body, she stood and surveyed the room as if there might be some resolution written on the wall.

There was a rag hanging nearby on a cabinet door, so she retrieved it and dunked it into a pitcher of cool water. Returning to his side, she patted at his heated forehead. When his tongue darted out to lick at his dry lips, she wrung a few drops of water into his mouth to moisten it.

Moments drifted into hours as she continued to minister to him the best she could. He awoke a few times, thanking her and reaching a hand towards her cheek but too weak to finish the movement. An ominous rattle from his chest occurred with each breath he took. She barely grabbed an empty pot in time for him before the vomiting started. When he had nothing left, his body continued to be racked with coughing and then dry heaving.

McKenna knew she was in way over her head.

"What the hell do I do?" She stood and twisted her hands in front of her. It was just afternoon, and before long, she'd have to think about her night flight, but she couldn't leave him.

"I'm fine. Don't do anything stupid." Surprised to hear him speaking, she looked to see him propped up on his elbows, gazing at her through half-lidded eyes. McKenna dropped to her knees beside him and took his hand to her chest.

"I don't do stupid things." *Except let myself fall for you.* "And you're not fine. You're sick."

"I can see the gears turning in your head." He paused to hack and cough. "Fuck, I'm gonna cough up a lung or something. Listen, I'm sick, I know. But promise me you won't do anything stupid. When night falls, take flight."

"Now how can I—"

"Promise."

His tone was forceful even in his unwell state. She nodded, placing his hand on his chest. "Fine. I promise."

And just like that, he was out again, head plopping down with a little thud. McKenna thought she too would be sick.

She could call on Roon for help, but there was enough suspicion surrounding her now and she didn't want to put any attention on her fae friend. Besides, she was certain that the safest thing for Robin would be to get him out of the faery realm. Maksim would come back, and since he couldn't hold weasel form, they would be in trouble.

McKenna stamped her foot and closed her eyes. With a deep breath, she reached out her hand and focused on Rooney's friend Jill. She'd seen her a few times when she and her boyfriend Doc stayed in the faery realm. They were her only connection with the human world.

The golden door opened and a very surprised Jill and Doc broke from an embrace to look at her with alarm.

"What the hell?" the man hissed, head down and eyes narrowed in wary concern.

"I'm sorry!" McKenna held her hands out to them. "You don't know me, but I've seen you and I need your help."

"You're McKenna," Jill spoke, gently shoving her man aside and approaching the golden door. "I recognize the cabin from our stay there. Am I right?"

A silly, giddy laugh welled up in her as she bobbed her head up and down, "Yes, yes. I'm McKenna."

Doc placed a hand on Jill's shoulder. "Are you hurt?"

When McKenna shook her head, Jill's eyes opened in alarm. "Roon and Belle? Are they all right?"

"No, no, it's Robin."

The bubbly blonde wrinkled her nose up in distaste and Doc grumbled something under his breath.

"You don't understand. He's sick. Terribly sick."

She stepped aside and motioned with her hand to Robin. As if on cue, his body lurched forward and he began coughing spasmodically.

"He's not a weasel anymore," Jill marveled. "How

did you do that? How did you make him a man again?"

"McKenna, how long as he been like that?" Impatient, Doc got even closer to the golden door, though not stepping through it.

"Hours, I suppose. I'm not sure exactly. Someone else found him. He was still in animal form. He's only gotten worse, and we don't get sick here, so I have no idea what to do. And if anyone finds out…" She lowered her voice, painfully aware that there could be Sentinel fae hiding on either side of the golden door and watching them.

"It's okay." Jill forced a smile. "Let me get Devan and we'll get you both here so that we can help."

CHAPTER 14

IT WAS DEVAN'S VOICE. He could hear her talking, but the words were distorted and impossible to decipher. Still, just the sound made him want to hurl and he wasn't sure why. He'd seen her one other time after she'd sent him to the faery realm, but something was different now.

He was different now.

He was also very sick. There was a deep pain down in his chest and it was hard to catch a breath. He coughed to try to open up the airways and the force of it shook the bed on which he was lying. He wasn't sure whose bed it was—or where he was.

Robbie clutched the headboard with both hands, head down and beads of sweat dripping from the hair at his forehead. "C'mon, baby. Give it to me. Harder…"

He didn't open his eyes to look at her, just kept moving, thrusting his hips again and again.

Devan was panting beneath him, moaning and trying to meet his demanding movements. Her tender hands were touching him, one grasping his shoulder and the other his back. They had attended a function at one of her father's charities that evening and she'd helped connect a few children from an orphanage to potential adoptive parents. She loved the children, ministering to them and helping them find new homes.

He always whisked her away for a wild romp on nights like these. She believed he was pledging his love to her. The Org thought he was being a stud, marking his territory. He knew it was something different.

This ritual was a sort of purge for him. Devan was all kindness and beauty and love. And after selling those children to the mercy of the Org vampires, he needed nothing more than to bury his cock in her goodness.

"Devvie…" he moaned, smothering his face into the pillow. "I can't, Devvie."

"Ugh, don't call me Devvie." A hand smacked his shoulder. "Did we have to bring him here?"

"Listen, I know there's some bad blood between you all, but he needs help. Isn't that what you people do? Help those who need it?"

McKenna. She was here with him. He instinctively tried to lift his hand and reach for her, but weakness made his limbs weigh about ten times too much. He groaned and rocked his head back and forth in frustration.

"You know, I remember something about weasels and the flu."

He recognized Jill's voice and confusion washed over him again. What the hell was going on? There was a pounding in his head, and he raked his hand through his hair before he squeezed his temples as if trying to collapse his own skull might help.

"It takes 'em down fast," Jill continued. "They die really quick. It's got to be the flu. I read about it in a book once."

"We need to get his fever down. He's burning up with 104.8 temperature."

"Give him some Tylenol then." Devan's voice was filled with rancor.

"No! Acetaminophen is dangerous for animals." Again Jill.

A strong hand grasped Robin's wrist, checking his pulse. "At the moment he's a man, Jill, and since I don't have any experience treating animals, that's about all the knowledge I have to go on. I'm going to treat him as a human for the flu. Get the bottle."

That was Doc Massey. The man could be adamant when he was treating a patient.

"Miguel, this is your fault. You take care of the doctor." Lucas was more than angry; he was boiling with rage. Robbie couldn't really blame him. The doctor

Lucas had his sights on had a huge trust fund. Upon granting him the chance, Lucas would become his sire and therefore the sole controller of all of that money.

The problem was, Lucas had changed the wrong doctor. Miguel had written down the wrong apartment number, transposing the digits, and the unsuspecting Alan Massey was not a vampire thanks to the blunder.

Miguel was a pretty good messenger when it came to transmitting verbal communication. Problems happened for him when it came to the written word; Robbie suspected he was dyslexic or something. When he looked at the Hispanic vampire, he saw a hungry glint in his eyes.

Miguel would enjoy killing the doctor, Robbie knew. He would take his time and make it as gruesome as possible.

"Remember that kid?" Robbie uncrossed his arms and pushed himself away from the wall. "The one with the broken leg?"

He could see that they remembered. Drake had not been more than eight when he fell and fractured his lower leg. But he was a firestarter, and no one could seem to get him to curb his magical abilities. Too wary of bringing him to a hospital, his vampire parents had tried to set the bone themselves. The kid had gone through a lot of pain and his injury never did heal properly.

"You mean Peg?" Robbie rolled his eyes and shook his head. Today Drake was an Org operative, but most

everyone called him Peg these days—short for Peg Leg.
"Yeah, that's the kid. If we'd had a doctor, I mean a
doctor working for the Org, he could've fixed him."
"You propose we use the doc? Instead of killing
him?"
"Why not? It could work."
Lucas rubbed his chin, thinking. "It's not a terrible
idea."

"It's a terrible idea. We can't keep him here." Devan's words broke Robin back out of his feverish dream. "I sent him to the faery realm as punishment. Why would I want to take him back in again?"

"He can't come back with me. If the Women find out about him, they'll know about the rebellion." Somehow the sound of McKenna's voice sent tendrils of relief through him. He didn't want to be back here with all of the ghosts of his past any more than those ghosts wanted him here. He needed McKenna there, close by.

"I didn't know there was a rebellion. How long has this been going on?"

"I don't know when it first started." They were sitting beside the fire after having eaten a hearty bowl of stew. Robbie was stretched out on the arm of McKenna's rocking chair, his furry tail hanging down the side. He almost purred when her soft hand dropped down to scratch him between the ears. There was nothing better than her touch on nights like these. "Aoi probably had

something to do with it, though she says the rumblings of a rebellion were there long before she arrived on the Island Anethemusa."

"What was the reason she was sent there?" He bent his neck, rolling his head up into her touch when she didn't immediately pet him again.

"She hasn't given me the entire story. I know there was a vampire. She meddled into some affair and the Women were displeased. She said there was something different about him—the vampire, I mean. But whatever it was that happened, it changed her. She's...she's like a woman in two halves. Part of her recalls something so sweet and beautiful that it makes her eyes look brilliant. Then most of the time she's all cold and hard and bent on the rebellion."

"Maybe she fell in love."

McKenna chortled. "I doubt it. You don't know my aunt. Love was a luxury she would never have taken the time for. She enjoyed her job as a Sentinel in the human world. She thrived on it."

"But you don't thrive on it here? Your job as a Sentinel."

"It's not the same in the faery realm. Over in your world, the bad, the danger, is so clear. Vampires who prey on fae. Witches with the power to bridge the two worlds without the oversight of the Women. Here, it isn't. Here I have a hard time stomaching that someone should be punished just for questioning the way of things."

He looked up at her, watching the way the fire cast

oranges and yellows against the smooth, golden skin. "But what will you get even if you are successful?"

"Freedom. Freedom not to spy on our people. Freedom not to have our wings clipped and our magic stolen for daring to think for ourselves."

"But what about your world? If the Women keep it in order, what will happen to it?"

"I don't know," she whispered. "I just have to trust Aoi about that."

CHAPTER 15

MCKENNA BIT HER LIP as she circled Gavin and Scilla's cabin. The place was quiet and dark, which was unusual this time of night. Scilla liked to dance, and Gavin would play the fife for her. They were a happy couple, and especially since the news of the baby, she wouldn't have expected their home to be silent.

With a sweeping movement, she sailed closer to the ground, careful not to lose the lift of the night wind. Nothing. No one was there. The scene was all too familiar, especially given the recent events with Hilda and her boys. The knot of tension she'd been carrying around since leaving Robin in the human world began to expand in McKenna's chest.

Her mind couldn't be swayed from thoughts of Robin. It had taken some serious discussion to convince Devan to let him stay. It was a little disconcerting to stand face to face with a woman who had once been his lover. Still, it was clear there was no love lost between them anymore.

Jill hadn't been excited about having Robin there either, but she at least hadn't been opposed to it. Jill and Doc had spent time with him at McKenna's cabin some time ago, so her willingness to bend hadn't been entirely surprising. For his part, Doc had tended to Robin with the utmost care. As long as they allowed him to stay, McKenna believed the doctor would do his best to make Robin well.

By morning, McKenna convinced herself that Gavin and Scilla had probably traveled to the Winter to see her parents. It was such a simple explanation that McKenna felt silly for even considering otherwise.

"Where's the rat?" Maksim stepped out of the shadows just as she dropped down off the wind and into the grass behind her cabin.

"Is there some reason you're spying on me, Maksim? Do the Women dispute my loyalty?"

He laughed, a cackling noise making her cringe inside. "'Course not. You're one of their best *slyphe* Sentinels. What would they do without you, McKenna?"

He was taking a jab at her, searching for any soft underbelly she might have. He always knew how to find the vulnerable spots. It was true that in her time as a Sentinel, McKenna had turned in countless fae for things the Women deemed infractions against the faery realm. She wasn't proud of it; she was in fact ashamed. Still, she did what she did to protect the Dissenters until they could rebel.

"I didn't see the weasel in your house. Did he run away? Who's going to keep that pallet warm for you now?"

He approached her and put his hand out, running his vile fingers along her arm. She fluttered her wings so that the air rushed at his face. Then, in the blink of an eye, she grabbed his wrist and twisted. "If the Women do not doubt me, then you have no business searching my house. Stay away from me, Maksim."

Bogle faeries weren't especially strong, but they had a unique power. They could melt their bodies into unusual shapes and forms. It allowed them to sneak into small spaces for spying. It also helped them escape capture.

Maksim's arms stretched like rubber and he slipped himself from McKenna's grasp. "I know you're up to something, McKenna. I can smell these things like a rancid animal's corpse in the river. I'll find out eventually."

With that, he turned to leave, detouring to the right of the cabin and kicking a mound of dirt beside a tree. She knew that was where Robbie stashed his nuts. Maksim was sending her a signal that he knew it too. He tossed her a backwards glance, and a shiver went down her spine.

Inside, the cabin was cold and lonely, like an empty cave. She missed Robin more than she could have thought possible and he'd only been gone since the previous evening. She yearned to check on him, but with Maksim so close, she couldn't take a chance on using her magic right now.

She took her sweater from the rocking chair and reached her hands into the arms. When she slipped the sweater on, she felt a scratching against her right arm and heard the crackle of paper. Her brow tightened into a frown, but before giving in to her curiosity, she searched the cabin for possible Sentinels and then latched the door and windows.

Satisfied, she tugged her right arm out of the sleeve and unpinned the note that had been left for her inside.

Nightfall plus five. The island.

Clearly Robin had reached the island and relayed the message from the Women, thereby sending Aoi into action. "So it begins," she murmured to the empty cabin. She was so exhausted that her body felt like it was moving through molasses. She had to get some rest for what lay ahead, but if her body was sluggish, her mind was on overdrive.

In a box in the corner of the kitchen, she located a small bag of dried roots. She traded the valerian with other fae in the Winter and Autumn sections where the plant couldn't grow. Until recently, she'd rarely needed help sleeping, but this morning was different.

Grinding up the oily root, she mixed it with some cold water then swallowed it down. She tucked herself between the covers on her pallet and waited for the herb to take effect.

It was afternoon before she awoke to a knock at her door. Groggy and fuzzy, she wiped at her eyes with the heel of her hand, crawling on her knees towards the door. She stood before grabbing the latch and opening it. A huge exhale released some of the tension still lodged in her chest.

"Scilla!" She took the woman's hands and leaned in to kiss her cheek. "What a surprise."

"Well, we wanted to thank Robbie for the pheasant he left for us yesterday. It was entirely more than we could finish so we shared it with Marcus and his family. And then Marcus and Gavin played some music so that the children and I could dance."

McKenna choked on her relief. "I was flying past your home and I saw that you weren't there. I thought perhaps you'd gone to see your parents."

Scilla giggled as she took the seat McKenna offered. "How did you know? We're leaving for Mother and Father's home today. Should arrive a few hours after dark. Where is your little pet? Is he out hunting again?" She scanned the cottage with glistening happiness in her eyes.

McKenna stoked the fire then placed a kettle over it to boil. "I'm not sure where he's run off to. I'm sure he'll be home soon. Tea?"

Scilla shook her head, hands waving, "No, I can't. I only have a few minutes. I wanted to bring this"—she held up a little knitted sweater—"for your pet."

"You made Robbie a sweater?"

"Well, when he stopped by, he had a chill. Even went into a bit of sneezing fit. I thought it would keep him warm when he's scavenging into the colder seasons."

Taking the offering, McKenna caressed the soft brown wool before smiling at her friend. "I'm sure he'll love it." There was a stab of guilt as she thought of how sick Robin was and wondered if it were her fault for sending him out across the seasons. The shortest crossing to Anethemusa was in the Autumn, which meant a very cold swim.

"I used the closest color I had to his coat. Wouldn't want to ruin his camouflage when he's out looking for game. Now I must go. Gavin will be ready to head off."

In a quick panicked movement, McKenna grabbed Scilla's hand. "It's late. Maybe you should leave tomorrow so that you can travel in the daylight."

A nervous smile jiggled at Scilla's lips as she slipped her hand from her friend's. "You worry too much, McKenna. We always travel in the evening. I get overheated in the sun, you know? This fair skin and red hair." She patted at her flaming locks then headed for the door.

Unease had McKenna's stomach churning. If Gavin and Scilla were traveling when the uprising began, they could run into trouble. The Sentinels that weren't a part of the Dissenters would sense the unrest in the country and would be looking for anyone who might be trouble. It would be much better for her friends if they remained home.

"Scilla!" She rushed the door, the other woman stopping to look back at her. Words failed McKenna. She gazed into the hopeful and lively green eyes of her friend and doubt crept into her soul. For the briefest of moments, she wondered if this revolt would really turn out to be the best for everyone. Swallowing back her fears, she forced a smile and a wave. "Safe journey."

CHAPTER 16

ROBIN LURCHED up in bed with a gasp and surveyed his surroundings. He was alone, not a single person there with him. The bed was soft and warm, and he appeared to be in what looked remarkably like a hospital. His body was achy and tired, and he was so thirsty it made his throat hurt when he spoke.

"McKenna..."

"She has gone back to the faery realm." The door opened and a huge man stepped into the dimly lit room, flipping a switch to flood it with light. He knew the face but couldn't recover a name from his muddled mind. The giant answered the unasked question. "I am Langston."

"The shaman," Robin croaked before clearing his throat. "I'm at Doc's hospital then?"

"Indeed. You were very sick."

"How long have I been asleep?"

"In and out for about twelve hours. Do not worry. Doc has his methods. I have my own. Between the two of us, I believe we will have you on the mend within a few days."

His mind was filled with cobwebs, and it was hard to string together any coherency. His eyes looked up, bobbing from point to point as he added hours, trying to calculate what time it would be. He knew faery time was a little different than human time, but he wasn't sure how. *Is it like the time zones and you add an hour or two?* he wondered.

"No time. I have to get back. We need to stop the Women."

"We?" The big man placed a hand on his shoulder to keep him from standing. "I believe you have much to tell us." He tossed a pair of pants and other articles of clothing onto the bed. "Let me get Devan and Kent while you dress."

Flipping back the blankets, Robin swung his legs over the side of the bed and then put his forehead into his hands, propping his elbow on his knees. He took the time to let his head recover from a bit from his fever. Then he hurried to put on the clothing Langston had provided.

When the door opened again, a crowd shuffled single file inside. He recognized Kent, Devan, Jill, and Doc, but another couple were strangers to him.

"This is Nicky and his wife, Gerry." Langston spoke with a soothing smile. "So now you have our attention. What has happened?"

"I want to know how the hell you're not a weasel anymore. You're supposed to be stripped of your powers."

Robin rolled his eyes at Devan and slammed his hands onto the mattress. "I know good and well what was supposed to happen to me, Devan. I know I was supposed to cross that threshold, lose my magic, and spend the rest of my days alone and miserable. I'm really sorry to disappoint you, but it didn't work out exactly like that." He wasn't sure where the anger was coming from. Maybe it was because he was so tired and still feeling sick. More likely it was because he was worried about McKenna and the inhabitants of the Island Anethemusa.

"Let's just chill, everyone." Jill stepped between Devan and Robin, putting her back to him and looking at her friend. He imagined that there was some unspoken message passing between the women. When he'd known them many years ago, they would communicate like that regularly.

Raking a frustrated hand through his hair, he gripped the locks in one hand for a moment and then rubbed his stubbly face. "Listen, we don't have time. The Dissenters need our help."

"We've already made a decision about what's happening in the faery realm, Robbie," Kent spoke, his voice level and calm. "After Devan helped Belle and Roon deliver Lodar to the Women, we all agreed." He motioned to the entire room. "All of us agreed that we wouldn't interfere in the internal politics of the realm. That was the purpose of the doors between the realms, to keep the two halves separate. Our focus is here. The Org is done and the Company is regrouping. Devan won't be used as a pawn."

"You don't understand what's going on. This isn't something that can be ignored. It's going to happen whether you like it or not."

"Whether I approve of all of their methods, the Women did help me at one time, Robbie. I'm not in a position to take sides, especially when I'm not even sure what the rebellion is all about."

"The rebellion is about absolute power, Devvie." Her eyes narrowed, flashing anger at him. He cleared his throat and began again. "Devan. The overthrow of the Sirens left the faery realm in the hands of the Women. It's true the gates were closed to isolate the faery realm, but that isn't all. Each time the Women send a fae through the gates, the magic doesn't just disappear. You all know your physics the same way I do. That energy, that magic, has to go somewhere. And it goes to the Women. The more power they have, the more they want, and that means the noose has to tighten more and more around the people. The fae are being sucked out of their existence and they don't even know it." These were all things he hadn't heard until just the day before. Aoi had given him an earful when he reported to her about Belle's communique with Fómhar. The woman somehow had known that all of this would be necessary to convince Devan and her friends to help the Dissenters.

OLIVIA HARDIN

"You're more ardent than I've ever heard you before, Robbie," Doc interjected. "But it doesn't mean I trust you. The question I have is: What's in this for you?"

Robin swallowed, his throat so dry that the action hurt. His eyes watered and he closed them tight until little bursts of color appeared. "Could I have some water or something?" The room got silent, but when he opened his eyes, he saw the giant move to the sink in long strides. He filled a paper cup and handed it to Robin. He drank it all down in one gulp before crushing the little cup in his palm. "There isn't an apology that I could possibly give that would excuse the things I've done to some of you. I could have asked McKenna or Roon to open the door months ago so that I could utter the words 'I'm sorry' but what good would it have done? It would have fallen on deaf ears because it could never be enough. You wouldn't have believed it anyway. But I am sorry. I'm sorry that I was such a shitty friend, Kent. I'm sorry I screwed with your love, Devan. I'm sorry I made Doc and Jill chess pieces in the Org's game."

"Well," Jill whispered, "in the end it turned out to be a pretty good game for me and Doc."

Devan cut her eyes at her blonde friend.

Standing, Robin approached the wall and slapped his palm against the cold concrete to lean himself against it, head down. "You want to know what's in it for me? My home. My life. My friends. My woman. I know I could have had all of those things before. They were right here in front of me and I threw them all away. But what I have there in that place is *all* that I have. And it's worth whatever I have to do to protect it."

He waited with bated breath, wondering what else he should say. He briefly wondered if there might be a spell or something to prove his honesty but shook his head at the thought. Soft steps approached him, and when he looked, he saw Jill's lavender eyes looking at him with intensity.

"I actually believe you, Robbie. But it doesn't mean I want to throw Devan or any of *my* friends into that fray."

"What about Roon and Belle? Or Devan's father, Daeglan? It's going to impact all of them."

"What exactly do you want us to do?" Kent questioned from behind him.

With a heave, Robin pushed himself from the wall and eyed his former best friend with optimism. "One of the Women, Fómhar, contacted Belle and told her that Báisteach intends to destroy the island. McKenna sent me to warn the island Dissenters. Aoi has a plan, but she needs help from this side, and Devan's the only one who can open the gate."

"Aw, fuck." For the first time, the dark-haired man, Nicky, spoke. He rolled his head from side to side as if arguing with himself and then turned his black eyes on Robin "What does Aoi have to do with this?"

Jill swung around, eyeing Robin and then Nicky with a confused frown. "You know a faery."

"Answer the question." Nicky's hands were fisted at

his sides. "How does this involve her?"

"Listen, you all know about the Island Anethemusa. Rooney and Belle told you it's the place where banished faeries are sent. Aoi has become the island's leader and therefore the leader of the Dissenters."

Nicky closed his eyes and gritted his teeth. He opened his mouth to speak again, but his wife beat him to the punch. "This means we're in then."

"The hell it does. It means *I'm* in. You're staying home with Emmie and Sophie."

"While you run off to save their grandfather's lover by yourself? I don't think so."

The couple seared each other with furious gazes until Langston stepped between them, touching each of them on the shoulder and gently pushing them a few steps away from each other. Robin was amazed by how quickly the tension between then dissolved.

After a moment, Nicky addressed the group again. "Aoi is the faery who saved my father and my mother the night he was changed into a vampire. He said she was forced to cross back into the faery realm. He didn't know what happened to her after that, but obviously she's on that island because of what she did for them."

"We'll bring her back," Gerry told him with a shrug. "If you want to keep her safe for your father, then we'll get her to cross over. Though God knows why we'd go to all that trouble when he has a perfect wife right here in front of him."

"Fine." Nicky nodded, though his face held a

distinct pout.

Robin turned to Devan, who was gnawing on the inside of her mouth in consternation. "Devan…"

She eyed Kent from the corner of her eye and he nodded. A huge rush of breath escaped Robin's mouth as relief washed over him.

CHAPTER 17

JUST BEFORE SUNSET, McKenna shoved her wooden chest from its place beside the hearth. Underneath was a long hole in the dirt covered with a scrap of wood. Inside, she recovered a long corkscrew-shaped silver rod with a crystal jewel in the top. Stuffing the rod into the arm of her tunic, McKenna took off for her night flight as normal and sailed the waves of wind to and fro above her sector. She caught sight of Maksim slinking around in the woods near the border of the Summer and Spring but, after giving him a few moments of inspection, decided he wasn't an immediate threat.

Continuing on, she gradually made her way to the place where she could breach her district and head in the direction of the Island Anethemusa. For the most protection, she flew east over the Cailean Lake before detouring north to the island.

Nightfall plus five had a specific meaning. In the faery realm, the stars were the same every night, without change. At exactly five hours past sunset, the brightest star in the fae sky reached its zenith. This would synchronize the Dissenters with a specific time to reach whatever rally point Aoi had for them.

Her skin itched with anticipation. She still didn't know how Robin was doing because she'd been too wary to contact him in the human realm for fear someone would catch her. He was safer there, she told herself. She had put him in enough danger by sending him off into the cold and almost getting him killed. He'd served his purpose. Now it was time to let him go.

Her heart rejected that thought almost before it was born. Somehow her companion had become more to her than just a means to an end. No matter who he had been before, Robin had devoted himself to her on every level. He risked his life each time he made a trip to the island and yet he did it always without question. It was true that she provided him a home and place to stay, but as she'd told him before, there were many of fae who would have taken him in.

McKenna didn't like the way thoughts of him tugged on her emotions, and she shook her blonde head in consternation. The stars were almost aligned properly, so she kicked her wings into high gear so that she could soar in the direction of the island. The wind chilled considerably as the combination of the colder seasons and the sea-blown air collided around her. By the time she landed on the island, her bones ached with the cold.

Aoi greeted her with an apathetic smile at the door of her cabin. The older fae draped a cape around McKenna's shoulders and then led her off toward the woods. "The fae will be gathering all over the realm. I alerted Rooney and Belle, but they are to remain in place until it happens."

"Until what happens? What is our plan?"

Aoi drew back, surprised. "Didn't the weasel tell you? He had clear instructions. He assured me he would take care of it."

The alarm behind Aoi's eyes was clear. It had never occurred to McKenna that Robin might have had an integral part to play in the actual rebellion. She assumed when she got the message in the arm of her sweater that he had completed his job.

A rush of hot and cold swept through McKenna's veins, and she frowned before speaking. "He became ill. He's in the human realm. I know nothing of any plans."

Her aunt swallowed and then brushed a palm across her graying auburn lock before straightening her shoulders. "We don't have much time. Based on our intelligence in the human world, the Sentinels haven't been able to keep tabs on the faery-witch and her companions when they are at that hospital... Is that where you took the weasel?"

For some reason, Aoi's consistent references to Robin as nothing more than an animal raised her hackles.

She tilted her chin up just barely and gritted her teeth before speaking. "He's at the hospital, yes. And you can refer to him as Robin. He isn't just a weasel any longer."

Aoi drew back though her expression remained stoic. Then she nodded. "If Robin is there, then he may have relayed the message, but we cannot be certain. But even in the case that he doesn't, we'll need to be prepared to get the island fae off of Anethemusa as soon as possible. If Báisteach means to destroy us, then I intend to set a trap for her."

"You've changed our original plans then? And I don't see how we can trap Báisteach when even her sisters cannot contain her."

A rare grin broke across Aoi's face. "Perhaps the Women cannot, but the faery-witch just might be able to. Your role is almost unchanged, except that now I want you to find a way to get Báisteach to Anethemusa."

McKenna took a deep breath, her mind churning with thought. "You're wagering much on the faery-witch. Do you think Devan will?"

"Aye, she will." An older faery stepped out of the shadows. He had long black hair and a salt-and-pepper beard. The gold-brown of his eyes reminded her of Devan's, and she realized in just a matter of seconds that this must be the faery-witch's father.

"You're Daeglan."

"I am," he nodded, a grim expression on a face marked with laugh lines that hinted to the fact that he was normally a jovial sort. "And my bairn will help us. She's a good soul."

McKenna recalled the woman she'd met just the evening before and wondered about that. She had no reason to doubt the goodness of Devan's soul, but based on her interaction with her, she wasn't so sure the faery-witch would really want to become involved in their problems.

Aoi barked orders to the Anethemusa fae as they exited their homes, pointing her finger and directing them as she wanted them. She barely noticed the golden door opening beside her, but McKenna was at full attention. Relief rushed through her when Robin stepped out first. The muscle moving in his jaw gave clear indication that he wasn't happy, but he met McKenna's gaze and gave her a little nod of acknowledgment.

Disappointment punched her in the gut, and she inhaled long and hard as she tried to tamp down the feeling. He'd been gone for a full day, and her lips longed to taste his. She missed him more than she could have thought possible, but she had to force herself to ignore those desires. They didn't have time for all of this emotion.

Several other people stepped out of the golden door behind Robin, though the only three she recognized by name were Jill, Doc, and Devan.

A gasp caught her attention, and she turned to see Aoi frozen in place, her delicate fingers held in midair close to her agape mouth. Her green eyes glistened with tears and her ivory face turned paler and ashen.

"My handsome..." Aoi whispered, and the way her

voice broke caused McKenna to fear she was about to pass out. Instead, Aoi rushed forward to stand before a dark-haired man. Both her hands rose as if to caress his face. Then they shuddered and held still without touching him.

The man had a rugged look about him, like someone unused to displaying affection or even kindness. He stared at Aoi a long moment. Then his expression softened and he took her hands in his, gently bringing them down to her waist. "No," he told her. "I'm not Viktor."

Aoi's body started to shake, and a sad smile crossed her face. The dark man must have sensed that her legs were about to buckle, because he walked her backwards to a large tree stump and helped her to sit.

McKenna wanted to rush to her side, but Aoi never allowed that sort of intimacy. It was a protective device so that the fae world wouldn't know or recognize their connection. Aoi had trained her well, and she stayed rooted to the spot even as she kept her eyes and ears trained on the scene.

"You must be Aoi," the man surmised, crouching down beside her, still holding her hands. "I think I've got a lot to thank you for. At least that's what my father says."

"Viktor? He's alive?"

He nodded, flashing her a smile. A woman moved in behind him, placing her hands on his shoulders. The look they exchanged spoke of an enduring love between them. "Viktor's alive. He told me all about you and how you saved him. I'm Nicholas, but call me Nicky. And this is my wife, Gerry."

Understanding clicked as McKenna heard the man's words. She knew why Aoi was here on the Island Anethemusa. She had been a *sylphe* faery living in the human realm and one of the Sentinels for the Women. She had broken her orders when she saved a new vampire from his sire. Aoi had been with many men in her long life, but she said that there had been something different about him. For him, she was sentenced to life sans her magic, in exile on the Island Anethemusa.

"We told him you were here. He asked us to bring you back. He wants you to be safe."

Aoi's eyes cut to the golden door, but there was no one on the other side. McKenna watched as her aunt took a deep breath, released it slowly, and then stood, recovering her hands from Nicky's grasp. "I won't leave my people. This is my duty, my campaign, and I won't give up on them." She motioned to the banished fae, watching with wide eyes.

Nicky's head moved up and down in curt acknowledgment. Then he turned back to his wife. "We asked. Now you need to go."

Gerry frowned and narrowed her dark eyes. McKenna knew an argument was coming even before the woman opened her mouth to speak, but Devan cut in. "Gerry, you said you'd go back. Don't make me force you through that door. The babies need you, and besides that, you have a job to do there. Kent and Langston are expecting you back."

The woman growled her displeasure, but she took a few steps toward the golden door. Just before she went through, she turned and crossed back to her husband, kissing his lips and whispering something to him. Then she moved through the golden threshold and walked back into her world.

CHAPTER 18

"THE MIGRATION is starting." A rough voice interrupted the moment, and Robin watched McKenna incline her head in acknowledgment when she noticed Clarence, her aunt's companion of sorts. He was a troll, which meant he was almost as wide of chest as he was tall. Still, he made a formidable form beside Aoi.

Devan caught sight her father about that time. He was stepping out of the shadows where he'd been speaking to some of the island fae. He embraced her, whispering something to her, then stepped away. "I'll be needin' to open the gate to Winter. Good luck, m'bairn."

Father and daughter exchanged a long look, affection so thick passing between them that it might have been visible on the air. Then Devan turned to Aoi. "Tell us what you have planned?"

McKenna must have only realized that introductions

were necessary because she quickly pointed out each newcomer by name before they proceeded further. Aoi acknowledged each with a nod, but her attention returned immediately to Devan. She assessed her up and down before she exhaled deep and smiled a frosty smile.

"Are your people tracking down my fae in the human realm?"

Robin suppressed a grin. The leader of the islanders was a formidable woman. She rarely answered a question straight off but instead insisted on asking one of her own before revealing her intentions.

"Kent and Langston, two of our team, will find them. Langston has the power to open the golden door, and he will let me know when they've got the crystals."

Looking to McKenna, Robin tried to discern what she knew about Aoi's plans. Everything the older faery told him was news, including the fact that the Dissenter fae in the human realm had been stockpiling a particular quality of quartz for decades. He didn't know why or how that fit into the revolution, but part of his message to Devan was a plea to collect and centralize those fae and their crystals at the hospital so that they could cross over.

Aoi smiled, stepping one leg out so that she held an Amazonian stance. "We have doors opening in each seasonal section of the faery realm. The island fae are migrating off the island and to their native sections. In a few hours, they'll track down their families and prepare for battle. And I hope that preparation will be for naught. I hope that you'll be able to stop Báisteach before it comes to that."

Devan's brow furrowed, and she sucked her lip into her mouth for a moment before speaking again. "You ascribe a good deal of confidence in me. What makes you think I can overcome the Women's powers?"

"I don't think you can overcome all of them, but I do think, with their help, you can overcome Báisteach. Her sisters know that she is a danger. Maybe Robin told you that Belle received a message from Fómhar."

"He told us," Jill piped in, glancing at him with a tenuous smile.

"If all of her sisters will side with us, I believe you can contain her."

"Contain? As in capture?"

Aoi took a deep breath, her expression as hard as ice and her green eyes stony. "Quite frankly, I wouldn't care if you killed her, but I assumed your sensibilities would reject that idea. And if that is the case, then I can wait to see her dead until after the fae place her on trial and execute her."

Aoi didn't wait to witness the reaction to that proclamation. She just turned to Clarence and gave more instruction. Robin continued to watch McKenna, admiring the beautiful flush in her cheeks. His ice queen was excited or nervous or both, but the reaction was lovely. It made it hard for him not to rush after her and take her in his arms. He knew she wouldn't approve, so he balled his hands into fists and crossed them behind his back.

"We have a problem. Ona hasn't opened the door to the Summer. We need to get that district's islanders away, and we're now behind schedule."

"I can open the door," McKenna piped in, stepping forward.

Eyes turning up to study the sky, Aoi frowned and shook her head. "We don't have that kind of time. Everything is perfectly planned and you must be in position—"

McKenna didn't let her aunt finish. "I'll rush them through. Robin knows Ona. He can try to locate her, and if he does, he can get her there to finish moving them through. My role won't matter if we can't get the islanders to the mainland."

Aoi considered this a moment, gazing at Robin long and hard. Finally she waved her hand dismissively and gave them the go-ahead. With a suck of air, he closed his eyes to transform from man to weasel. He was still weak and tired from his illness, but whatever the shaman had given him to drink just before they'd left the hospital had done the trick.

"C'mon." He tromped up to McKenna, waiting for her to open the golden door. She paused, and he gazed up at her with intense green eyes. She smiled before she reached down to pet him, rubbing her hand from his head to his tail. He couldn't help curling his back up into her touch.

McKenna opened the door and a crowd of fae rushed forward. Before they could start milling through the gate,

Robbie scurried through with urgent intent. The door opened into a cave, and it took his animal instincts just a few seconds to click into gear and give him his bearings. He ran as fast as he could towards Ona's home.

Aimilíona was one of only a handful of Dissenters who hadn't at one time been a Sentinel. Her advantage was that she was young and beautiful and perfectly innocent. Still, behind her pleasant demeanor was a shrewd woman who kept a keen eye on things and found a way to impart what she knew to Aoi's people on Anethemusa.

Maintaining her cover was also easier since Ona's brother, Aiden, was a bit simple. She could excuse her wandering because she so often had to run out to look for him. And Robbie knew it was true the boy did roam the countryside as there were a few times he'd seen it necessary to coax him back when he found Aiden far from his home.

When he approached her cabin, he first caught sight of Aiden, the young fae's backside up in the air as he rooted under a downed log, probably searching out some sort of critter. He lurched up with a start, rubbing the tip of his nose and then sneezing a few times in quick succession.

"Find something?" Robbie asked.

The young man, probably about twenty in physical age but only about seven mentally, grinned and his head bounced up and down in the affirmative.

"'Twas a baby squirrel. It kicked dirt in m'nose and I sneezed."

Robbie stopped and stood up on his hindquarters, rolling his claws round and round each other. "Yep, I saw that. Bless you." Aiden looked confused, and Robbie wondered if maybe fae didn't use that custom in this realm. "It's a little late for you to be out. Is your sister around?"

"Had a visitor."

Concerned, Robbie scampered up the wall so that he could peek into the window. Ona was alone, pacing the room with a worried look. Sniffing the air, Robbie slipped in to the house then scanned and inspected every nook and cranny for Sentinels. When he was sure the place was safe, he hurried to Ona, who was now crouching and waiting for him to come close.

"Who was it?"

Aimilíona ran a shaky hand through her white-blonde hair. "Maksim. He left about thirty minutes ago but I was so afraid he might be lurkin' about that I didn't go to the rendezvous point. Have they started?"

"Yes. McKenna is holding the gate open now, but it seems Aoi has another job for her, and I'm to fetch you if you can come."

Ona nodded. "Yes, let's go."

Robbie's claws scratched against the wood floor as he hurried to the door. "I'll stay behind a bit and keep an eye out for Maksim or anyone else."

CHAPTER 19

T HE CAVE was getting crowded as the summer islanders filled all of the tunnels and enclaves. Most
of them carried knives, swords, or some other form of
blade. Each of these was made of the purest iron that
could be forged. Iron was deadly to faeries, and because
the islanders had no magic, this was their only hope of
protection.

Everyone was bubbling with excitement for the moment, and why wouldn't they be? Many of these fae
hadn't seen their friends and families in years, and even
with the threat of revolution, the positive vibes were pal-
pable. McKenna kept one eye on the golden gate, antici-
pating Aoi's warning for her to move on to the next
phase. The other eye she kept on the exit tunnel, waiting
for Robbie to come back, hopefully with Ona and Aiden.

"Hilda..." McKenna breathed the woman's name

when she saw her cross into the tunnel. Her son Donte was close behind her. "It is so good to see you."

Hilda's eyes filled with tears, which she quickly wiped away with a sigh. "It is good to see you too, m'dear."

Direon was noticeably missing, and McKenna's green eyes bored into Donte's, seeking an answer. He dropped his eyes and shook his head, squeezing his mother's shoulder. "He fought them, McKenna. He refused to give his wish as they demanded and he tried to attack Maksim. I suppose he has much of our father in his blood, as his rebellious nature is what led to his demise as well."

Demise. The word sent a chill into McKenna's veins. Keeping her attention on Hilda, she reached a hand out and rubbed the woman's arm, extending what comfort she could.

"McKenna!" She turned to see Ona rushing her, embracing her before motioning her brother Aiden off to a group of kindly fae.

"Oh, it's so good you're here. I need to get going."

"I know. I'm so sorry. Maksim was sticking his nose into things and I had to be careful before coming."

"Robbie?"

"'E'll be along in just a few moments," Ona told her with an assuring smile. "He was keeping an eye out lest someone follow me."

"It is time," Aoi spoke from the other side of the door. "You must go now if you have hopes to be there before sunrise."

McKenna inclined her head to acknowledge the order. Then she released the gate to the island and opened one to the yard just in front of her cabin. Tension coiled in her stomach and churned up her esophagus, threatening to make her sick. She swallowed and then skulked off through the woods, doing her best to look suspicious.

For all that Maksim showed up when she least wanted to see him, it was almost comical that he wouldn't find her quickly when she did want to get caught. As luck would have it, a little gang of wood elves located her first. All five of the tiny men were almost identical in looks, about half a foot tall with scraggly gray beards and white hair. She knew them to be the Billybong brothers, a sobriquet derived from the forest they inhabited. The fae didn't generally have surnames.

Elves might have been small, but they could be powerful. At least McKenna hoped the Billybong brothers were as strong as she had been told. It would do no good for her to get caught by a weak band of Sentinels. Her capture had to look un-staged.

"A little early for you to be on your feet, eh, McKenna."

McKenna halted before them, fisting her hands and raising her chin. "I delivered someone to the Women and had to leave the night wind. I'm completing my duty on the ground."

One of the little men laughed. "There are strange happenings in the faery realm this night. We've seen nothing amiss yet, but we smell it. Like a dog on the hunt, we know something is happening."

Rolling her eyes, McKenna waved her hand at them in dismissal before she tried to detour around them. "Keep your eyes open. I'm sure you'll find something."

The elves moved fast to surround her again. She flashed an angry frown at them and it wasn't an act. She was angry because they needed to just get on with it and take her to the Women. "Clear out of my way, little men. I don't have time for games."

"And what sort of game are you playing, McKenna?"

Maksim. She didn't have to turn to see him. The sound of his voice sent tremors of discomfort down her spine. The Billybong brothers snickered, raising their hands to unleash a veil of magic to drape over her.

McKenna both dodged the net and also fluttered her wings to blast a wave of magic that would send the net flying back towards the elves. The little men scattered, fussing as they went. Before she could turn to face him, Maksim was behind her, clutching her hands in an unbreakable hold and forcing her down onto her knees. He might have been shorter than she, but he wielded enough strength that she didn't have to feign his overpowering her.

She was surprised when his knee connected with her ribs, the air bursting from her lungs along with a cry. She tried to wrestle away from him, but he came around to her side, still holding her hands with one of his, and grabbed her by the hair, forcing her face down into the dirt.

"You're been a haughty little witch for a long time, McKenna. I'll take great pleasure turning you over to the Women. But first…" He yanked her head back and then bashed it down against a rock. Pain exploded just above her eye, and after a moment, she felt hot blood dripping down and obscuring her gaze.

"Maksim. She is subdued."

It was Winn's voice, the faery who escorted captured fae to the Women. The Billybong brothers must have opened the door so that he could deliver her to the Women. Relief swept through McKenna's limbs in waves. Maksim tried to pull her to her feet, but she was woozy and couldn't get her footing. Strong arms lifted her and carried her.

After a few steps, she was deposited on a hard, rocky surface her hands tethered in front of her with rope. When she finally recovered her senses, McKenna opened her eyes and saw stone that she knew well to be the grey hill where the women resided. Glancing up through her uninjured eye, she saw that the Women were listening to the Billybong brothers give their dissertation of the events leading up to her capture.

While attention was still averted from her, McKenna clawed at the ground to start a hole large enough for the silver rod she'd stuffed into her sleeve. The stone of the hill was hard to get through, and she had to heave and push the pointed end with all the strength she could muster just to drill it deep into the surface.

"And what have you to say, McKenna?" Báisteach demanded, streams of waters originating from her eyes beginning to seep into the ground below her.

McKenna made sure to hide the rod with her legs as she stood. She faced all four Women with shoulders back and hands fisted. "I lost my lift on the night wind when I slipped too close to the ground. That is why I was wandering on foot."

"And yet you lied to us," Earrach whispered, her voice heavy with sadness.

Even feeling as she did about the revolt and the need to break the noose of the Women, the tone of Earrach's voice pierced McKenna's heart. These Women had been her world's overseers, their mother figures, their goddesses.

"But the truth is that her service has been impeccable all this time. Must we make an issue of this?" Fómhar huffed with a flick of her brown hair.

"Have you grown soft, sister?' Báisteach growled, floating towards McKenna on a cloud. "Her actions are traitorous. She must be dealt with. But first, I want to know what she was really about. I find it hard to believe a *slyphe* faery of her years could fall from the wind so easily."

A cold, wet wind blew into McKenna's face and she shivered but remained standing tall. Her head throbbed from the blow Maksim had dealt, but except for the blood streaming into her eye, she was able to mostly ignore it. Still, when Báisteach drew close, almost nose to nose, she had the urge to shrink away. It took all of her strength to stand solid and meet the powerful woman's gaze.

"Tell me, McKenna. What are you up to? Don't tell me you are planning to revolt against your guardians."

CHAPTER 20

BY THE TIME Robbie scampered back to the cave, he found that McKenna was already gone. A sense of foreboding niggled the back of his mind, but he tried to push it away. He was exhausted from running after Ona and keeping the Sentinels off her back. He found his discarded clothing in a corner, probably placed there by McKenna, so he released his hold on the shift so that he could return to human form.

"Well, well." A female voice caught his attention just as he was slipping into his pants. Jill approached with a grin then pursed her lips and whistled. "So you can do that little trick all by yourself, eh? I kinda thought maybe it was something McKenna did to make you shift."

Robin took a deep breath and leaned back against the stone cavern. "Nah, it wasn't her. I don't really know how it happened. It just did. One day she mentioned she saw some spark of energy in me. Then I could make myself change from animal to man. Lately..." He paused and considered things. "I didn't realize it until I got sick, but lately the man form is the one my body wants to stay in. It's an effort to make myself a weasel and it's hard to hold when I'm this weak."

When he looked at her, he saw Jill standing with her arms crossed, eyes serious, but a slight upturn of a grin on her lips. He rolled his eyes and let his body slide to the floor so that he could prop his forearms on his knees.

"Sorry. I know you don't care about this. I know this wasn't what you guys wanted to happen to me."

"Hey." She shrugged and walked a little closer to him. "I'm not the one who made the decision to banish you here. Truth is, you're lucky Devan was your judge because I was in a bad way fighting the vampire darkness, and I woulda killed your ass on the spot."

He flinched and rubbed his eyes.

"But I've realized things aren't always what they seem, Robbie. Coming here and spending that time in this world made me believe that I could change my thinking. And if I could change, then I guess it isn't a huge leap that you could too."

"Necessity taught me a little humility, but that doesn't change the things that happened," he whispered. Robin craned his neck when he saw someone approaching then inclined his head as Doc came up behind Jill. He placed a hand on her shoulder, drawing her back towards him.

The blonde gave her lover an adoring smile before she turned back to Robin. "Here, it is what is. If you're more natural as a man again, it's because something has changed. Otherwise, you'd still be just a weasel."

Nodding his head, Robin crawled his way back up to his feet. "Are you two the only ones here?"

"Nicky and Gerry are with the Spring. She finally wore him down and convinced him that Langston, Kristana, and Viktor could take care of the babies. I understand Rooney and Belle traveled to his parents' home in the Fall so they are there waiting for the explosion. Daeglan is in the Winter with Kent, and we're here, so that means each sector is covered so to speak. Aoi's of course on the island with Dev."

It didn't seem like much of a plan to Robin. After all of their plotting and subterfuge, it felt a little insufficient to just send the magic-less islanders to their family and hope that they could drum up enough power and help to overcome. He knew Aoi hoped this would be merely a coup of sorts, but something told him there would be more of a backlash than just Báisteach's wrath.

He watched Jill and Doc walk slowly away, lost in conversation together. His tired mind wanted to shut down and sleep, but he couldn't seem to put on the breaks. After a moment, he reconsidered Jill's words and alarm bells sounded. "Explosion? Jill," he called to her, "what do you mean the explosion?"

The blonde turned to him and cocked her head to the

side. "The hill, of course. Langston delivered the crystals just before we shut down all of the doors. If all goes as planned, they'll be able to focus the sunlight to the hill —"

"McKenna," Robin breathed, palming the cave wall to push himself forward. "She's on that hill, isn't she?"

Jill couldn't seem to speak. She just held her hands out in helplessness, her eyes wide. Robin didn't wait for her to come up with a response. He shifted immediately back to weasel and took off in the direction of the hill.

Inwardly, he shook his head in frustration. How could she have kept this from him? All the times they'd talked, gone over all that the Dissenters were involved in as they prepared for the revolt, she never once mentioned this part of the plan. How long had she known? Had she always intended to give herself up to the Women?

Maybe someday they will take the wrong fae up to that hill. Maybe one day it will all be a trap and it will be the end of their reign.

She had been protecting him. He was sure of it. There was no other reason for her deception. McKenna had seen things in him that others didn't. She had found a reason to trust him from the first moment she saw him. That trust had only grown to the point that she'd granted him access to her body and her heart. If she had chosen to keep this part of the rebellion from him, then it was because she expected things to go badly for her.

He picked up his speed, racing through the countryside and crossing boundaries toward the gray hill. The horizon was beginning to glow pink, and he knew that sunrise was approaching. When he reached the silent plateau that was the home for the Women, he wasted no time running up to the apex. Even before he reached them, he could see and hear what was happening.

"There are things worse than death, McKenna. What is the meaning of your betrayal? Tell us now."

Báisteach levitated on a cloud just in front of McKenna with one clawed hand extended to her neck. The Woman wasn't physically touching McKenna, but a blaze of magic from her hand held his lover in an iron grip. He could see that her hands were tied in front of her and she struggled to free those bonds.

"It isn't me you'll need to worry about," McKenna panted, her face splotchy and red. "Aoibhneas and the islanders are going to rise up—"

"No!" Robbie screamed at the same moment he shifted back to a man.

Báisteach released McKenna, dropping her to the ground. The Woman shrieked and laughed as she floated up higher into the sky and then blew towards the Island Anethemusa in a ball of light and water.

CHAPTER 21

"WHAT HAVE you done?" Earrach wept, dropping to her knees and holding her face in her hands.

McKenna took a moment to recover her breath before she raised her tied hands to touch her swollen and blood-caked eye. When she looked up, she was amazed at what she saw. As long as she had reported to this hill, the four seasonal Women had always remained in their own quarter of a perfect circle in the ground: Earrach, the Spring; Samhradh, the Summer; Fómhar, the Autumn; and Geimhreadh, the Winter.

Now Fómhar took a step out of the circle. A shimmy passed through her body and her eyes rolled back in her head for just a few seconds. Then she recovered and locked her gaze with McKenna. "I hope for all of our sakes that this was the right decision." Then she opened a door, stepped through, and was gone.

Earrach began to cry all the more, collapsing farther into herself until she was in a fetal position. Geimhreadh huffed the breath from her mouth, sparkles of ice accumulating in a cloud in front of her. Then the white-haired woman reached out to wrap an arm around her sister in comfort.

Samhradh stared at McKenna with an intense fire. She too left her circle, experiencing the same vibration of energy through her body, then approached them. From the corner of her eye, McKenna saw Robin approach and place himself between her and the Woman.

"McKenna is one of mine, Robin. I am of the Summer, as is she. I mean her no harm." Then the flame-haired Woman flicked her wrist and McKenna's bindings dissolved.

"Our family is destroyed then," Geimhreadh said. "Lunacy, betrayal, abandonment. We will not be whole again."

Samhradh issued a sad smile and inclined her head. "Our world will not be whole, at least not for a long time. But then, it hasn't been for a many, many years."

All sense of normalcy, if it could be called that, in the faery realm dissolved then. It wasn't a physical change. It wasn't something they could hear. It was just an overwhelming sense that things were spinning irrevocably out of kilter.

Samhradh followed her sister's lead, summoning the golden door, then left the hill. McKenna felt the warmth of sun touch her back. She shivered and turned to Robin. "We need to get out of here. Now."

But when she tried to open a door, she found that only a spark of golden light appeared in front of her before it fizzled out. Panic welled up in her, and she wondered for a moment if her powers had somehow been stripped away. Then, when she tried to stand, she turned dizzy and faint. She realized it must just be the injuries making her powers so weak. Concentrating harder, she finally manifested the door and started to usher them both through it.

"No," Giemhreadh spoke low, her voice cold as ice. She pointed her finger at McKenna's door, ice crystals forming around the edges until the opening was closed. "You aren't leaving until you tell me what will happen to my sister. You've set a trap for Báisteach and—"

A beam of light flooded the top of the hillock, blinding them. Giemhreadh curled her arm over her eyes, crying out. Robin cursed and averted his gaze down.

"Shift, Robin! Shift now!"

She was relieved when he didn't waste time asking questions. He just closed his eyes in deliberation. His body shrank down to his weasel and she scooped him up into her arms. With a deep breath and eyes closed, she ran at the edge of the plateau and dove off.

The wind was only slight, but the momentum of her fall provided enough airflow to give her lift. She fluttered her wings as hard and as fast as she could, using every ounce of energy and air to glide as far from the gray hill as possible.

And then the sound of an explosion rocked the world behind her just as her feet were about to touch ground. She glanced back in time to see a shockwave of rock and crystal and energy running towards her. McKenna ducked behind a huge tree, rolling into a ball with Robbie cradled close to her bosom. The air and debris sailed past them, sandblasting her arms and back. The minutes passed in slow motion as she waited for the detonation to end.

Robbie wriggled in her arms, and she sat up so that he could get free. He scurried away from her and then transformed back to human form. He brushed dust and stones from his hair before he crawled to her, grabbing her behind the head and crushing her lips with his. The kiss was demanding, but it somehow filled her, replenishing her where injury, exhaustion, and strain had left her weak. Warmth and strength surged in her veins as she clutched him, drawing him as close to her body as she could.

Tearing away from the kiss, she caressed both side of his face and then nuzzled her forehead to his. "I love you."

Robin chuckled, pecking her nose. "I know you do." He took a deep breath. "And just in case that was a little too arrogant, you need to know that I damned well love you too. You are the first and the only woman I have ever really loved." He drew back and looked at her, touching the goose egg on her head with a frown of derision. "I should kill those bitches for doing this to you."

She swallowed. "This wasn't the Women. This was Maksim."

"That fucking Napoleon-complex little freak. I *will* kill him."

There was movement behind them, and McKenna looked around Robin to see some of the fae taking tentative steps into the open, their gazes alarmed and a bit thunderstruck as they stared at the place where the hill had been.

"Maybe I'll let you kill him later, Robin. For now, this isn't over yet."

"I was afraid you'd say that."

And she stood, lifting him up with her. Bending at the waist, she grabbed two large pieces of the quartz stone that had been at the center of the cold, gray hill. She approached a young faery woman and handed her a piece. "Take this. Tell the others. You may need it, but only one. None of us needs more than one." The crystal was the catalyst that allowed the Women to absorb and restrain the power of the banished fae. The destruction of the hill would end that process, hopefully for good.

She took a breath, hoping it would cleanse her anxiety, but a knot was still tight in the pit of her stomach. Still, she opened the golden door, grabbed Robin's hand, and led him through.

They stepped into her cabin and she immediately reached for a pair of his trousers from the wardrobe. Robin said not a word as he accepted the offered clothing, dressed, then turned to her in askance.

"How much magic do you think you have?" she asked him, approaching and taking his hand so that she could place it over the quartz in her palm.

He looked confused, his brow furrowing tight. "I don't know. I haven't tried to use more than just shifting."

She inhaled raggedly, her eyes wide and glistening. "I can wish you some of mine. We don't know what lies ahead and I don't want you to be defenseless."

Robin drew his head back cupped her bottom hand with his, and squeezed. "But that's not what you are supposed to do, is it?"

"The island fae will find their loved ones and will collect a crystal. A simple wish can restore part of the magic those fae lost. That's what the quartz can do—focus the magic."

He grinned, at once a sad and happy expression. "Give it to Aoi, McKenna. I have you. You've come this far and we're not going to deviate from the plan now."

CHAPTER 22

ALL WAS EERILY QUIET when they arrived back at the Island Anethemusa. Far in the distance, a flickering glow signified the smoldering remains of the gray hill. Robin's eyes scanned left and right, all his senses alert to danger lurking somewhere in the absence of sound. The absence of people.

"Where are they?" he asked, following McKenna as she approached a little clearing just opposite Aoi's cabin.

"I don't know. Maybe it's over. Maybe."

Robin didn't think so. His hackles were up, all of his nerves sparking in anticipation of something. And whatever that something was, he was afraid he'd be damned well helpless to stop it. Finally in his life he had someone worth taking care of and he was all but powerless to protect her.

"Do you hear that? It's like a buzzing sound."

McKenna's head bobbed up and down. She fluttered her wings and a blue light surged through the veins, lighting them up with energy. She took several more steps, sucked in a breath, and motioned him down. He followed her direction, crouching low and searching with his eyes for the source of the noise.

"There's a little mound and then a crater that drains towards a cave."

"Yeah. Let's go."

She led the way, walking with her waist bent a little to keep her head down. As they got closer, they could see a green, blue, and yellow glow. The colors burst and pulsed and flitted as if something extreme was happening on the other side of the mound. The droning sound got louder and Robin realized it wasn't just a steady sound but it was also ebbing and flowing along with the colors.

"Shit."

Robin uttered that word, rushing forward when he saw the scene laid out before them. Devan and Báisteach were engaged, both of them flinging energy balls. The intensity in Devvie's eyes was so familiar that his heart felt literally pierced with remorse.

They stood face to face, circling with arms outstretched. She pointed a palm at him and shot an orb of icy energy, disappointed when it merely fizzled upon striking his chest. He did his best to give her full display of the confidence in his eyes. He wanted her to wilt so that this would all be easier.

"You must have thought I was a fool, Robbie. You and my father, dragging me along with your nasty business. Did he order you to date me? To get me involved in the business? To keep an eye on me?"

Robbie laughed, his green eyes glistening with ugly delight. "I don't take orders from anyone, especially your father. He works for us."

Devan dodged the channel of red-glowing energy he poured towards her with his palm. He was impressed, so he amped things up a bit and the next round of magic grazed her arm and side. She dropped to her knees in pain, and he immediately regretted the action. He didn't want to hurt her, just subdue her so that he could get her to the Org. Worried, he rushed at her to inspect her injury, but she fought and tried to get away. She dove to the side to avoid him, rolling into the dirt.

Robbie fired another red wave of magic at her, and she surprised him when she conjured a concave shield to deflect the burst back at him. With a rush of air, he managed to duck just in time.

"Very good, Devvie," Robbie mocked, ignoring the stinging pain in the small of his back where he fell onto a rock.

"Don't call me that." Hissing the words, she flung her head forward in his direction. Jagged crystals of ice landed a blow to his chest and tossed him backwards, the shards shattering all around. "You don't take orders,

*huh?" she smiled, panting with exertion and also exhil-
aration as she started to gain the upper hand. "I think
you take orders from him." She cocked her head towards
Adriel.*

*Robbie was losing control. Devan's magic was cir-
cling him, pushing him backwards against a huge tree
trunk. Confusion draped a cloud over his mind as he
struggled to come up with some sort of countermeasure.*

*"What's the matter, Robbie?" she demanded in a
whisper as she used her power to hold him in place.
"Why are you taking orders from a vampire, selling your
own kind for a profit? Do you know what that makes you,
Robbie? It makes you a man-whore."*

Robin shuddered with the memory as he watched
the clash between the two women. Devan was brilliant,
the intensity of her actions awe-inspirng. She swung her
arms out in turns, flashing balls of icy power at Báisteach. The faery-witch and the water Woman were fairly
matched as neither was yet gaining the upper hand, both
parrying and striking equally.

When had Devan become that woman? When had
she found the strength and the determination to take on
someone as powerful as one of the Women? He remembered the girl he'd dated, how she'd always put others
before herself. She took on people's problems and made
them her own. Instead of admiring those characteristics
when she was his, he's derided her as weak. He knew
now that she was anything but.

Frustration with his own failings chewed at him, and he had to look away from the spectacle. When he averted his eyes, he caught a glimpse of graying red hair and looked to see Aoi, her back to them. First she was standing, but then she slumped forward, finally dropping to her knees all in the space of a few seconds that lasted hours.

Robin reached out to grab McKenna's attention and watched as Aoi tipped face forward. Her falling body revealed that of Maksim standing in front of her, and the glistening blood on the blade of a dagger in his hand was clear.

"No!" McKenna screamed, lurching upright and running to her aunt's side. Robin followed her, but his attention was not on the slain faery. He only had eyes for Maksim.

The nasty slug of a man harrumphed as he glanced at McKenna, who was crying. He wiped his blade on the leg of his pants and looked at Robin with a challenging gaze. Maksim was just like all of the men he'd worked for all of his life. Those who preyed on the ones who were weaker than they were. And he'd helped them acquire and even subdue their victims. He had *been* one of them.

Robin didn't even realize what was happening until he saw the glowing blue in his hands. The power of magic in the palm of his hand was thrilling and frightening at the same time. It had been so long since he'd felt this sort of power that he almost didn't know what to do with it.

But when Maksim sneered and took a step closer to McKenna, he hesitated no more. With a growl, he pressed his palm forward and let loose the energy stored at his fingertips. The troll cried out and fell backwards, hurrying to stand. Robin let him get to his feet before he struck him again, this time firing from the other hand.

This magic was different than the power he'd had before. It exploded in bombardments instead of searing with heat. Alternating hands, Robin beat the short faery back a few steps each time until he stood on a precipice that dropped into the crater where Devan and Báisteach were fighting.

Eyes wide, Maksim looked down. When he saw how steep and dangerous the drop was, he scampered to get away from the edge. With Maksim's attention down, Robin advanced and grabbed the little man at the back of the neck. When Maksim tried to lunge with his dagger, Robin was faster and turned the troll's wrist back on him so that the blade dug deep into his abdomen.

"Who are you?" Maksim gurgled, coughing and spitting up blood.

Robin didn't deem the question worthy of an answer. He just let go of him and watched as he tumbled backwards into the pit, his body coming to rest about ten yards from the still-battling Women.

"Robin!"

It was McKenna calling to him, so he abandoned all thoughts of the slain troll and returned to her side. She was clutching the wound in her aunt's stomach, but blood was pooling fast all around.

CHAPTER 23

DEVAN, ROBIN, MCKENNA, AND AOI were all back at the hospital in the human realm. It hadn't been easy to get Devan's attention during her battle with Báisteach. The faery-witch had fought with an intensity. Once she'd disengaged, Báisteach had drawn back as if exhausted, giving Devan the time to open the door so that they could get Aoi to the hospital.

Inwardly, McKenna felt sick at the thought that perhaps Devan could have permanently ended Báisteach's reign if only given the time. Still, even that wasn't worth it if Aoi's life could be saved.

While the shaman Langston tended to her aunt, McKenna allowed Devan to apply some of her healing power to the injury above her eye. The wound didn't go away completely, but the swelling all but disappeared and the gash sutured itself closed.

Langston approached them with downcast eyes. "The knife was pure iron. This troll knew what he was about. Perhaps if I could have treated her sooner, I might have been able to keep the poison from entering her system. As it is, she cannot be saved. I am sorry."

So it had all been for naught. Aoi was dying. Her mind understood, but her heart wasn't willing. "Oh, no, please!" McKenna begged, eyes flicking from Langston to Robin. "Robin brought us here because he said you were the best. She cannot die. She can't!"

The giant reached out to place a hand on her shoulder, and though her heart was breaking, calmness settled into her limbs. "You have a few moments," he told her.

Everyone began to shuffle out of the room, but the warmth of Robin's body coming up behind her was a comfort. He placed her hand on his shoulder, and she rubbed her cheek against it. "Want me to stay?"

"No. Let me have a minute."

Aoi's eyes were closed, and though her clothing was caked with blood, the wound was taped and no longer openly bleeding. McKenna took her hand, shivering because the fingers were so cold and stiff. Her aunt opened her eyes and forced a dry-lipped smile.

"It's over, isn't it?" Aoi whimpered, tears welling in her eyes. "I've failed."

"No, you didn't. It isn't over. It won't be over until we're free," McKenna insisted, her expression hard.

"How can I be sure? My plan may have been awry. It may have been flawed. I've worried. I've had doubts that made me want to run and hide. No. No. No. Is this what the people want? What have I done? They are ignorant. They are blind. Open their eyes. We must open their eyes."

The broken woman lying on the table was like no one McKenna had ever seen in her aunt. She was panicked, crazed, unsure. This was not the leader of the island fae. This was not the patriot who would save her world from despotism.

"Listen to me, Aoi. Listen!" She shook her aunt's shoulders. "We will win this. Our world will be free. I promise you it will be free."

And then the strong Aoi returned in an instant. "You did well, McKenna. No plan ever turns out perfectly, but your role was flawless. You may be proud."

All McKenna could do was nod her head, swallowing back emotion.

"You care for the weasel? For Robin?"

She couldn't keep the surprise from her expression. Drawing back, she reached a hand up to rub the cut above her eye. "I do care for him. I love him."

If she'd been surprised before, McKenna was stunned when Aoi's lips parted and she released a sob. Her eyes welled with tears, and she tugged weakly to pull her niece closer. "If you love him, do not ever let him go. No matter what may come, no matter how you are threatened. Face it together, never apart. Love him as long as he will love you in return."

"Okay," McKenna told her, patting her hand for

comfort. "I understand. I will. I will."

"No, you listen. You must listen. The revolt is a noble idea. It is good and right. I know that it is. Revenge is an act of passion; vengeance of justice. Injuries are revenged; crimes are avenged. Justice. Justice. Justice." Aoi sputtered and coughed a moment before continuing. "But none of it matters as it should without love. Love makes all the difference."

McKenna was crying now, choking sobs breaking from her lips. She shuddered and clutched at her aunt's fingers, rubbing as if she might be able to replenish the heat and life draining from Aoi's body.

The two women embraced, both of them weeping together. There was a tap on the door. McKenna sniffed, wiped at her nose, and then turned. A tall and handsome older man stepped into the room, stuffing his hands into his pockets as if nervous.

"I am very sorry to interrupt," he said, his voice full of gravel. "I just…" He sucked in a breath. "Please, may I see her?"

She wasn't sure why it happened, but her sobs started again and she reached a hand up to cover her face. "You're Viktor."

"Viktor," Aoi whispered.

McKenna held her aunt's hand tighter when the woman began trembling uncontrollably. She peered at Aoi, love and affection glistening in her eyes, then petted her graying red back from her face. Kissing the ghostly pale cheek, she turned to Viktor and motioned him forward.

He wasted not a second and crossed the room in only three long strides. When he was there, McKenna took his hand and placed her aunt's within it. Then she backed away to the far corner so that they would have privacy.

She couldn't hear the words, but for just a few moments, Aoi came back to life just a little. She sat up on her elbow, clutching at Viktor. The love between them was so thick that both of them transformed when they were close to one another. They were younger, they were softer, they were one.

Then all of a sudden, the air left her aunt's lungs and her body became slack. Viktor slid both of his arms under Aoi's body and tugged her into his chest. Her arms hung limp, moving without life as he rocked her, petting her hair and crying into her neck.

McKenna raised her eyes to the ceiling, tears falling in hot streams down her cheeks. Her legs went weak and she dropped back against the wall, letting her body sink to the floor. Wrapping her arms around her knees, she rocked herself back and forth as the realization that Aoibhneas was dead.

CHAPTER 24

R OBIN FOUND MCKENNA on the floor of the hospital room, her arms wrapped around her bent knees and her cheek against her forearm. She gazed blankly in his direction, though not focusing on him or on anything else. He approached her slowly, part of him afraid of the fractured look behind those green eyes. She somehow reminded him of his mother in those early days, before they'd made a pact with the Org, when she still had enough soul to feel bad about the way things were.

"Is she gone?" he asked, his heart pierced with a jab of pain when she jumped as if frightened.

"Yes." Her whispered response was so soft it almost didn't register in his ears at all.

This last job had been a big one, and Robbie should

have been proud of it. The kid he'd tracked down had been a runaway, which was harder to come by than those already in the orphanage/foster home system. Those kids were ripe for the picking, but when a magic child was discovered out from under that umbrella, most of the Org didn't even bother with that kind of trouble. Robbie knew that this boy was different and he intended to make sure the trouble had been well worth his while.

The lights were on in the spacious condo he shared with Veronica. It wasn't surprising. She was a vampire, so she rarely slept at nights. She loved the lavish surroundings his job with the Org provided. She attended parties, rubbed elbows with the very wealthy, and most importantly, she had magic blood to feed upon almost whenever she desired.

Even though he wasn't surprised to find the house alight, Robbie sensed something was off the moment he walked in the door. The hairs on the back of his neck rose with a twitch and he instinctively fisted and unfisted his hands in preparation of something lurking behind the door when he stepped inside.

"Ah, Robin, you are finally here, my boy. I was told you'd have a nice morsel for me. I have been waiting for some time."

Lodar was what the women called handsome, and Robbie figured he could see why. He had the classic Roman look and the confidence to go along with it.

"I didn't know you'd come here for the child. I intended to bring him to you later this evening."

"Ah, no." He made a smacking noise with his tongue against his teeth and shook his head. *"I heard how exceptional this one is supposed to be. I couldn't wait to sample. Please, where is he?"*

With a deep breath, Robin stuffed his hand into his pocket for his keys. "Give me just a moment."

The boy, Craig, was asleep in his back seat. He'd given the child an herb tonic to make his sleep, mixing it with his drink when he finally talked him into a meal. Something about the boy's eyes had told him that he'd had suspicions about what Robin was up to, but for whatever reason he hadn't fought.

After delivering the sleeping child into Lodar's arms, Robin went in search of his mother. He found her in the theater room, curled into a ball with one of her vampire lovers, Sam. They were both asleep, satiated smiles on their faces. There was a girl, about fifteen, watching a movie on the recliner in the corner. She grinned up at him and then focused her attention back on the show. Robbie knew she was a supplicant as well.

Hours passed and Robbie waited there with the girl, unsure whether he should interrupt Lodar. Vampires were persnickety, and this one was known to be the worst. After a time he stepped in the hallway and looked up just as the vampire entered the room.

"You've done well, boy. Much better than I might have expected. You deserve something special. I will pay you well, indeed double what I promised. But I also have a bonus."

With captivated eyes, Robin watched as Lodar crossed the room and came to stand above Veronica and Sam. Like she was his own lover, Lodar reached down to caress Veronica's hair, brushing it back from her face and humming low as he did so. Then, without warning, he grabbed her at either temple and twisted her head, snapping it from her body in one swift movement.

Horrified, Robin watched his mother's eyes opened wide in alarm just before her body burst into a heap of ash. He heard himself cry out, though he wasn't sure why. Maybe because it was the right thing to do. Veronica Weir was the one who'd given him life. Still, in the pit of his soul he knew the truth. He knew that he was better off now without her.

Lodar's bonus to him was a life without the albatross of his mother around his neck.

McKenna sniffed and rubbed the heels of her hands into her eyes before turning her eyes up to him. Robin's chest constricted with sadness for her. He reached his arms around and helped her to rise and then walked her from the room in slow, short steps. Devan and Langston were there waiting in the hallway. He tried to smile at them but failed.

"I am sorry," Devan spoke, approaching McKenna, compassion heavy in her gaze.

"Can I go home?"

He flinched when she spoke the words because McKenna's voice sounded so unlike her. Eyes wide, brow furrowed, he leveled Devan with a questioning glance.

"Of course. I will open the door whenever you're ready."

"I want to go home."

The door appeared before them, and Robin led her across the threshold, afraid that she would collapse if he didn't help her. She followed but then stopped when they appeared in front of her cabin. Shrugging her shoulders to get away from his touch, she took a few steps and then halted again to tilt her head back and examine her world.

It was around midday, but the sky was filled with dark clouds. A fierce wind whipped leaves and sticks along the ground. Robin knew this wasn't what the Summer was supposed to be like. A feeling of déjà vu washed over him as he recalled the events from earlier that year when Báisteach first lost control.

When he focused his attention back to McKenna, it was with the intention of asking her what action they should take. The woman he knew, the one he'd come to love over this past year, would have immediately set her mind to something that should be done, some errand he should run. The crushing pressure behind his breastbone increased when he watched her shoulders sink and her head drop. Without a single word, McKenna walked into the cabin and closed the door.

$\mathcal{E}$PILOGUE

BÁISTEACH STOOD ATOP the highest peak on the Island Anethemusa and gazed out in the direction of the mainland. Her arms throbbed with exhaustion and long tendrils of her hair had worked loose and were whipping around her face with each gust of wind. She did not cry, though for the first time in a very long while, melancholy filled her. She couldn't afford the tears. Her energy might not be replenished for some time, so each drop of her life-giving water must be conserved.

Mentally, she reached out to her sisters. Fómhar was totally blocked to her, as was Samhradh. She pressed harder, seeking entrance to their minds, but unable to breach their walls. It occurred to her with some regret that they had blocked themselves from her some time ago. She wasn't sure when, as she hadn't cared enough to know. That was a mistake. If she'd kept better tabs on them, she might have recognized the signs of the uprising much sooner. She would be more careful in the future.

Earrach was open to her, but the misery and pain in her sister's thoughts and feelings was too much for Báisteach. This was no time for despair. Still, she knew her springtime sister better than all the rest perhaps, and it was clear to her that Earrach would not emerge from her sad place for some time yet.

Báisteach turned then to Geimhreadh. A shiver passed through her body as she touched her sister's mind. The Winter Woman was livid, her fury and resentment brimming over. Hard, cold resolve was settling in Geimhreadh's soul, and Báisteach knew she had found her one and only ally—for now at least. Tendrils reached out from her mind and sought the people of the Winter district. The Women could not intrude in the minds of their people, but they could sense minute impressions through the connection with the seasons. Geimhreadh was in the Winter with her fae, and through her, Báisteach could get a taste of what was happening.

Confusion, anguish, fear, even traces of joy.

"Yes," Báisteach murmured to herself. "I can work with those. They can be the seeds."

I am coming to you, sister, she spoke mentally to Geimhreadh.

And I am waiting, sister. Come.

Rising up on a cloud, Báisteach flew in the direction of the Winter district. She paid little heed to the movement of thousands of fae on the ground. She didn't need to. She knew well what was happening. The banished-island fae were reconciling with their families. All of the wishes that had been used to ease the hearts of her people would be undone and uncertainty would prevail in the faery realm.

All because of a few dissenters. Dissenters and the meddling faery-witch. Báisteach had known the moment the faery-witch was born that she would lead to troubles in the faery world. If she'd been wiser, she would have kept Devan's powers tethered forever so that she might never have risen to become so powerful. Better yet, she could have had the woman killed when she was just a child instead of having her followed. Another mistake, she knew. Still, she had needed the faery-witch to secure her justice against Lodar The price, it seemed, had been higher than she'd imagined.

But Báisteach could rise again. As life for her people became more and more unsettled, that would lead to overall unrest. And unrest would eventually require the people to search for a leader. And she would emerge for them again. She would be the one they came to for help. And she would embrace her children, her followers loyal at heart. And those children would once again rise to stamp out the disturbing forces in their world.

They would make the faery realm one of peace and tranquility and perfection once again.

It was unfortunate that it would come to this. After all they'd been through to reach this time of harmony, to have it unraveled now was shameful. To make matters worse, they would have to go through reconstruction without the help of Fómhar and Samhradh.

Her sisters would have to be the first to go. Only when Fómhar and Samhradh were dead would the heirs to their powers be born. It was the way of things. The bad, the wicked, and the evil would be stamped out, their bodies returned to the good earth to give life to successors who could put things right.

And always Báisteach would be at the forefront. Her people would want her there. She was the giver of life, the bringer of water and renewing power. That would always be here role. Because…

Here, it is what is.

ACKNOWLEDGMENTS

Maybe it isn't fair to name him in the dedication and the acknowledgment, but it's my book so... I need to thank my husband, Danny for all the answers, the ideas, the historical evaluations. You didn't even know I was picking your brain at the time, but you always made time for my incessant questions and hypotheticals. To my editor Mickey Reed for her time and work to make this book shine. And then Tawdra Kandle for giving it the last go through; I know your time is so very precious and I appreciate all that you do for me, both as my friend and as my associate. Thank you Stacey Blake for making my books so pretty; it isn't easy to hand over the reigns but you so far surpass my abilities that it is an honor. Of course the ladies of Romantic Edge Books because when I'm down you pick me and, when I'm lost you show me the map and when I'm feeling silly you laugh with all my goofiness. And last, but certainly not least, to all of my readers; you are the most important part of my journey. Thank you each and every one.

About the Author

When Olivia Hardin started having movie-like dreams in her teens, she had no choice but to begin putting them to paper. Before long, the writing bug had bitten her, and she knew she wanted to be a published author. Several rejections plus a little bit of life later, she was temporarily "cured" of the urge to write. That is, until she met a group of talented and fabulous writers who gave her the direction and encouragement she needed to get lost in the words again.

Olivia has attended three different universities over the years and toyed with majors in Computer Technology,

English, History and Geology. Then one day she heard the term "road scholar,'" and she knew that was what she wanted to be. Now she "studies" anything and everything just for the joy of learning. She's also an insatiable crafter who only completes about 1 out of 5 projects, a jogger who hates to run, and she's sometimes accused of being artistic.
A native Texas girl, Olivia lives in the beautiful Lone Star state with her husband, Danny and their puppy, Bonnie.

Connect with Olivia and Get information about releases, contests, news and more here:

Website: http://olivia-hardin.com/

Blog: http://oliviahardinwriter.com

Newsletter: http://eepurl.com/m13aj

Twitter: http://twitter.com/oliviaH_writer

Facebook Fan Page:
http://www.facebook.com/oliviahardin

"This war will be over in a month."

Robin's words might as well be my own; I can definitely remember stories of people believing different wars would end in short order. Specifically I recall the movie *Gone With the Wind* when Scarlett marries Charles Hamilton and he tells her, "Don't cry, darling, the war will be over in a few weeks." Poor Charles was as much a fool for believing Scarlett's tears were for him as the North and South were to believe the war would be over quickly. The conflict in fact lasted almost four years.

So, thinking of all of this made me want to do a little research on the subject—I am, after all a "history nerd."

In July 1861 the first encounter of the United States Civil War took place when Northern troops entered Virginia at the First Battle of Bull Run or First Manassas.

Accounts from the engagement indicate that "innumerable" civilians followed US troops out of Washington, taking with them picnic baskets of food for the trip. It's frequently suggested that these people wanted to see some of the war before it was over, because surely it was to be over within no more than a matter of months.

William Howard Russell, a *London Times* correspondent of the time notes the following:

> *The spectators were all excited, and a lady with an opera-glass who was near me was quite beside herself when an unusually heavy discharge roused the current of her blood—"That is splendid. Oh, my! Is not that first-rate? I guess we will be in Richmond this time to-morrow."*

Similarly, the First World War is sometimes referred to as "the war that would be over by Christmas" because that term was bandied about often. That conflict actually lasted from 1914 to 1918.

One might even consider George W. Bush's so-called "mission accomplished" speech on May 1, 2003 during the Iraqi war. At that point the war wasn't even a year long. The White House insisted Bush's speech was not a declaration that the war was over, though many criticized him for the mere suggestion. In the end, the Iraqi War continued until 2011 when the US formally lowered the flag there.

Whether Robin's premonition about the revolt in the faery realm will prove to be a short-lived conflict or a drawn-out war will remain to be seen. But don't worry, I promise to do my best to get that book into your hands in "a few months."

Happy reading, All!

~Olivia

OLIVIA HARDIN

A DANGEROUS
Season

FOR LOVE OF FAE TRILOGY - BOOK 3

Sneak Peak at A Dangerous Season
(For Love of Fae Book Three)

"She doesn't like it."

"Of course she does."

"Bullshit. She damned well hates it."

"Don't use that language around my daughters."

"She hates it more than the hat." As if to prove her mother's point about how much she despised her new big pink headband, Emmie turned beet red and howled her displeasure. She kicked and pumped her fists at Nicky in angry jerks, gasping for breath between frantic wails.

Gerry couldn't contain her mirth, laughing out loud even as she switched Sophie from the crook of her arm to her shoulder.

Nicky slipped the band off of the baby's head, then lifted her close to his chest. "Aw, c'mon Emmie-baby. Don't cry. Daddy's sorry."

Gerry snorted and reached a hand out to caress the fussing infant. "You do realize crying is okay for her, right? Works her lungs and makes her strong. Don't act like it's the end of the world every time she screams. It isn't necessary to make a spectacle of yourself over it."

"Mommy's mean, isn't she. She's the meanest mommy in the whole world. My poor Emmie-baby."

Gerry rolled her eyes and slipped Sophie into her basinet, careful not to disturb her sound sleep. Stuffing her hand into the diaper bag, she found one of the pacifiers and reached over Nicky's arm to pop it into the crying baby's mouth. She jiggled it back and forth a moment before Emmie latched onto it and started sucking hard. Within seconds her eyes were closed and her breathing was slowing.

There was a little tap on the door to the nursery and Gerry wasn't surprised to see Joya poking her head around the corner. The auburn-haired woman grinned sheepishly and tip-toed in, her hands tight against her stomach. "I heard the crying. I thought I would check."

Raising an eyebrow, Gerry cut her eyes in Nicky's direction. "Why am I not surprised? Everyone makes fools of themselves over these babies."

Nicky bounced Emmie a few more times, then handed her into Joya's waiting arms with a half-grin. "How's Viktor?"

"Oh," Joya's loving smile wavered ever so slightly as she thought of her husband, "He will be well. He just finished some breakfast and is in the study with the tall-man."

The tall-man was Langston, Gerry was sure. It had been weeks since Viktor held the woman he had once loved in his arms as she died. The effect on him was profound and Gerry knew Nicky was worried about his father. She thought it was a bit strange, considering the two had only met each other a few months before that, but then her Nicky was nothing if not loyal.

"Do you mind sitting with the twins?" Gerry asked Joya, knowing immediately the answer. Viktor's wife might not be blood related, but she'd taken to surrogate grand-motherhood as if she were born to it. That too was strange, since she was probably not more than ten years older than Gerry herself. Joya nodded, grinning her red-painted lips, then turned back to the infant in her arms.

As they walked out of the room together Nicky gave her a cocky grin and she knew exactly what he was thinking. A little twist of worry coiled in her stomach. Motherhood wasn't exactly something she had planned... at least not yet. The birth of her girls was a blessing, but perhaps a curse as well. She loved the babies, but she was awkward and unsure of herself in the role of parent. And more than that, her mind and body twitched to be back on the job and into the fray.

"You look like you need a cigarette."

Rolling her eyes Gerry swept her hand out and smacked him. "If you pick up a cigarette I'll kick your ass."

Nicky laughed, then suddenly turned his head to the side. They two of them were not just husband and wife, but an efficient team and she knew well and good by the look on his face that he heard something. Her senses immediately went on high alert.

"Let's check out the south wing," he flicked his thumb in that direction and they both turned.

The hospital had become home to all of their team, Devan and Kent, Jill and Doc, Langston and Kristana, Nicky and Gerry and of course all of the rescued Org children. It was fortunate that Doc and Jill had had so much time on their hands years before. The building was spacious and refurbished for comfortable living. The different wings were established into separate living quarters, with Langston and Kris remaining in the wing with the children.

Gerry wasn't sure she'd like the arrangement forever, but for now it provided the best of all worlds for them. A safe, comfortable home, constant babysitters on the ready and also a means of keeping tabs on all of the action.

Since things had mostly settled down with the Org, the current action was the recent rebellion in the faery realm. Of course Nicky had nearly kept her out of that initial skirmish. She got to do a little sparing when the revolt broke out, but then the fae all retreated to their corners to regroup and Nicky insisted they had to come home to their babies.

They reached the end of the south wing where Doc and Jill spent most of their time. It was grey outside the doors, the sky cloudy and threatening rain. Nicky placed his palm on the lever, but didn't depress it to open the door just yet. Instead he put his ear close and listened.

Releasing a deep sigh, he shook his head and glanced over his shoulder at her, "I thought I heard a cry, but now I think it just sounds like the kids."

A twinge of disappointment rolled over her and then she too shook her head, though not about the children. She wondered when she'd become so anxious for excitement that she actually *wanted* them to be under attack. "We might as well check on them."

Nicky pushed the door open and they both hopped down the steps into the rear yard of the hospital. They both looked left, right and then left again but there were no signs of any of the children. The grounds were deep and wooded, but they should still have been able to see the children if they were close enough to hear.

"Maybe they're playing hide and seek," she offered, brow furrowed in thought. Then she saw a twinkling flash in her peripheral about the time Nicky turned swiftly in the same direction. Langston had strong protections placed all around the perimeter of this hospital and in the distance those wards were flickering and blinking as if something was trying to get through.

Nicky and Gerry reacted instantly, both taking off at a run. He was a dhampir, which meant he was super-fast like a vampire and so Gerry knew he would get to the protection boundary first. She fisted her hands, imaging her own magic pooling into her palms then sent out mental feelers in search of whatever attacker was there. She couldn't feel one single person, but many small blinking flashes of consciousness.

"They're fucking pixies," Nicky cursed when she reached him. She narrowed her eyes and ground her teeth. She didn't need his explanation since she could clearly see the dozens of fluttering faeries just beyond the wards. Every so often a pixie would advance and try to get through and the protections would spark to life. "What the hell do you guys want?" her husband demanded, shooing at them with his hands as they swarmed into a group just in front of him.

"We need the faery-witch. We need help." They spoke in unison.

Coming June 2014

ROMANTIC EDGE BOOKS

Meet the authors of Romantic Edge Books: Nine Authors Writing Romance with an Edge

Anthologies
Cupid Painted Blind
Once Upon a Midnight Dreary
Eternal Summer
A Christmas Yet To Come

By Olivia Hardin
Bend-Bite-Shift Trilogy
Witch Way Bends
Bitten Shame
Shifty Business
For Love of Fae Series
Sweet Magic Song
Lynlee Lincoln Series
Trolling for Trouble
Tangled Up In Trouble
Stand Alone Novels
All For Hope

By Liz Schulte's
Guardian Trilogy
Secrets
Choices
Consequences
Be Light: A Christmas Short Story
Easy Bake Coven Series
Easy Bake Coven
Hungry Hungry Hoodoo
Pickup Styx
The Jinn Series
Ember
The Ella Reynolds Series
Dark Corners
Dark Passing
Stand Alone Novels
The Ninth Floor

By C. G. Powell
Spell Checked
Immortal Voyage
The Miss Series
Miss Stake

By Lola James
Spell Bound Series
Bound to Remember
Unbound
Bound to You
Fate Series
Fate's Design
A Villain's Fate Short Story
Defying Fate

By Stephanie Nelson
Gwen Sparks Series
Craved
Deceived
Coveted
The Anna Avery Series
Taming the Wolf
Embracing the Wolf
Stand Alone Novels
Turning Home (A Small Town Novel)

By Melissa Lummis
Love and Light Series
Enlightened
Samskaras
The Little Flame Series
Coming March 2014

By Tawdra Kandle
The King Series
Fearless
Breathless
Restless
Endless
The Serendipity Duet
Undeniable
Stand Alone Novels
The Posse
Best Served Cold

www.ingramcontent.com/pod-product-compliance
Lightning Source LLC
Chambersburg PA
CBHW060423130626
46555CB00005B/2183